A PARTRIDGE AND A PREGNANCY

WILLA NASH

A PARTRIDGE AND A PREGNANCY

Copyright © 2021 by Devney Perry LLC

All rights reserved.

ISBN: 978-1-950692-92-7

This is a work of fiction. Names, characters, places and incidents are the product of the author's imagination or are used fictitiously. Any resemblance to actual events, locales or persons, living or dead, is coincidental.

Editing & Proofreading:

Marion Archer, Making Manuscripts

www.makingmanuscripts.com

Karen Lawson, The Proof is in the Reading

Judy Zweifel, Judy's Proofreading

www.judysproofreading.com

Julie Deaton, Deaton Author Services

www.facebook.com/jdproofs

Cover:

OTHER TITLES

Calamity Montana Series

The Bribe

The Bluff

The Brazen

The Bully

Holiday Brothers Series

The Naughty, The Nice and The Nanny

Three Bells, Two Bows and One Brother's Best Friend

A Partridge and a Pregnancy

———

Writing as Devney Perry

Jamison Valley Series

The Coppersmith Farmhouse

The Clover Chapel

The Lucky Heart

The Outpost

The Bitterroot Inn

The Candle Palace

Maysen Jar Series

The Birthday List

Letters to Molly

Lark Cove Series

Tattered

Timid

Tragic

Tinsel

Clifton Forge Series

Steel King

Riven Knight

Stone Princess

Noble Prince

Fallen Jester

Tin Queen

Runaway Series

Runaway Road

Wild Highway

Quarter Miles

Forsaken Trail

Dotted Lines

The Edens Series

Christmas in Quincy - Prequel

Indigo Ridge

Juniper Hill

CHAPTER ONE

EVA

I'm pregnant.

"Nope," I muttered. There was no way I'd be able to say those two words out loud. Not yet.

Maybe tomorrow, but definitely not today.

My insides churned as I stared at the house in front of me. This was not where I wanted to be standing.

The cold was becoming unbearable. My nose was probably as red as Rudolph's by now. There was a very real chance I'd lose my pinky toe to frostbite if I stayed out here much longer. I should go. Back to the car. Up to the door.

Yet here I stood.

Stuck.

I'd planned to spend my Christmas Eve at home, lounging in my flannel pajamas in front of my gas fireplace with a cup of cocoa in one hand and a book in the other.

Instead, I was frozen to the sidewalk in front of my one-night stand's house, working up the courage to ring the doorbell and announce I was pregnant.

I'm pregnant. Oh, how I wished those two words would stop bouncing around my head, and instead, bounce out of my mouth.

But first, I had to get unstuck.

My car was parked in the driveway at my back. Driving across town hadn't been an issue. Neither had putting the sedan in park and stepping out from behind the wheel. I'd even managed to walk to the sidewalk. Twenty feet separated me from my destination. But my shoes might as well have been ice blocks in the concrete.

How had it come to this? How was I even here? I'd asked myself the same questions hours ago when I'd been sitting on the bathroom floor with a positive pregnancy test in hand.

One night. One night with Tobias. A farewell.

And now I was pregnant.

Stupid freaking farewells. Though technically, it had been *another* farewell.

Tobias and I had met for a drink to catch up. There'd been a little flirting. A lot of cabernet. When he'd asked me to come home with him, I'd decided it was fate giving me a second chance to say goodbye.

Our first goodbye hadn't gone so well. There'd been crying—me. There'd been angry silence—him. There'd been heartache—us.

Over the years, I'd thought a lot about the night Tobias and I had ended our relationship. I'd replayed it countless times, wondering what I should have done and what I should have said.

Regrets had their way of ambushing you during the quiet moments.

So six weeks ago, I'd seen an evening together as my do-over. We'd spent the night laughing and talking, reminiscing about times past. And in true Tobias style, he hadn't disappointed in the bedroom. It had been a one-night stand to set things right.

Why did one-night stand sound so cheap and sleezy? Tobias was neither. He was handsome and caring. Witty and charismatic. Loyal and steadfast.

Our night had reminded me just how wonderful he was. And maybe he'd remembered too, that once I hadn't been the villain. Once, I'd been the woman he'd loved, not the woman who'd broken his heart.

We'd had our second goodbye. The perfect goodbye. Yet here I was, knocked up and about to say hello.

"Oh, God." My stomach roiled. Was it too soon for morning sickness?

I didn't know shit about pregnancy. I didn't know shit about babies. I didn't know shit about being a mother. How was I supposed to raise a child when I couldn't even traverse a sidewalk, ring a doorbell and spit out two words?

This was Tobias. It wasn't like I was telling a stranger. He knew me, possibly too well, which made this terrifying.

There'd be no hiding my fears. No stalling the uncomfortable conversations. There'd be no raising my chin and pretending this was no sweat.

One step. Just take one little step.

I lifted a foot. And put it right back down in the snow print where it had been.

Maybe I could write him a note? My hands were shaking so badly I doubted I'd be able to hold a pen.

The pregnancy test was in the pocket of my red parka. Maybe I could just drop the pee stick by the door and make a break for it, like that teenage prank where kids put dog poo in a paper bag, lit it on fire, rang the doorbell and ran like their lives depended on it.

Not that I'd ever done that prank.

Being the getaway driver and waiting around the block for my friends didn't count.

My chin began to quiver.

Why was this so hard? Why couldn't I move?

Thank God, Tobias didn't have neighbors. They probably would have called the cops on me by now.

Come to think of it . . . it was too bad he didn't have neighbors. Because if the police showed up, I could just give them the pregnancy test and ask them to deliver the news.

Damn Tobias and his country house.

I'm pregnant.

Just two little words. One sentence. *Say it, Eva. Just say it.*

I opened my mouth.

Nothing. Just a puff of white air.

This trip was pointless. I should have stayed home and paced. After I'd missed my period, I'd started to worry, but as a self-proclaimed master-of-avoidance when it came to my personal problems, I'd dismissed it as stress.

Moving was always stressful, no matter how often I'd relocated, and I'd been busy gearing up for London. But avoidance could only last so long, and this week, when another day had passed without my cycle and my boobs felt as tender as my favorite medium-rare filet mignon, it had been time to face reality.

I'd gone to the nearest grocery store, picked up a pregnancy test, rushed through self-checkout and scurried home to pee.

The world had stopped spinning when the word pregnant had appeared in pink letters on that white stick. I'd clutched it to my chest while I'd sat on the bathroom floor for an hour. Then I'd paced.

An apartment void of all furniture gave a girl a lot of room for walking. So much so, that I'd paced for two hours. Then my feet had carried me to my car, which had led me here.

Whatever courage I'd had on the drive over had evaporated. And now I was stuck. I hadn't been this stuck in years.

My hands wouldn't stop shaking. Tears welled in my

eyes. How was I supposed to do this? Not just tell Tobias, but what happened next? How was I going to be a mother?

I was seconds away from collapsing in the snow and giving in to a good cry when the door to his house whipped open. And there he was, standing tall and broad, filling the threshold.

"Eva, what are you doing?"

I glanced at my feet.

"You're standing there," he answered for me.

I nodded.

"It's been thirty minutes."

That long, huh? Now it made sense why I was so cold.

"Are you going to knock?" he asked.

"I'm not sure yet." I gave myself a little fist pump for actually verbalizing a thought. Progress. This was good. Words were good.

"It's cold."

"Yeah. You should go inside. I'm good here."

"Eva."

See? This was the problem with Tobias. He could look at me and know I was very, very not good.

"Come inside," he ordered.

"I can't."

"Why not?" He stepped off his stoop and onto the sidewalk. His long strides ate up the distance between us, and when he stopped, he towered over me. "What's going on? Is everything okay?"

I shook my head. "I'm stuck."

He blew out a long breath, then he fished my right hand from my coat pocket, cupping his fingers to mine so our thumbs were opposite. "One. Two. Three. Four. I declare a thumb war."

I closed my eyes so I wouldn't cry, then said the next words. "Five. Six. Seven. Eight. Try to keep your thumb straight."

"I win, you come inside."

"Okay," I whispered.

"Shake." He touched his thumb to mine, wiggling it up and down. Then he pinned my thumb beneath his because I didn't put up a fight.

We both knew I needed him to be victorious.

This was how our thumb wars had usually gone. He'd instigate. I'd surrender.

And as he clasped my hand tighter, giving me one gentle tug, he unstuck my feet.

The warmth in the entryway was like stepping into a sauna after being outside for so long.

Tobias closed the door behind us. "Want me to take your coat?"

"No, thanks." I stuffed my hand into the pocket again and wrapped a fist around the pregnancy test. Later, after I'd dropped the bomb, I'd tell him he'd better wash his hands.

"Would you like to sit?" he asked.

I lifted a shoulder in a noncommittal shrug.

Would he hate me for this? Maybe in the past six

weeks, he'd found someone else. A woman he *chose* to have a baby with. That thought made my pulse pound behind my temples so I shoved it away.

"Eva."

My throat had closed again.

He sighed and took my elbow, steering me toward the kitchen where he pulled out a stool for me to sit at the black quartz island. Then he rounded its corner and leaned against the far counter to wait.

He waited.

It was one thing I'd always loved about him. Tobias never rushed me. My sister would have gotten so annoyed by the silence that she would have given up outside in the snow. My father would have asked question after question, badgering me until I talked.

In my youth, I'd needed Dad to push me until I'd confessed how I was feeling. About school. About friends. About Mom. But I wasn't a teenager anymore dealing with an absent parent and adolescent drama.

Tobias knew if he pushed, I'd crumble.

Why was I like this? At the moment, it wasn't the most important question but it seemed to scream the loudest. At work, I never got stuck. Never. I always knew what to say. What to do. Which was possibly the reason I loved to work and dodge anything resembling a personal conversation.

Would our kid be patient like Tobias? That question sent my stomach into a tailspin. We were going to have a baby. Would he be mad if I puked on his fancy wood floors?

I squeezed my eyes shut, willing the nausea to pass. It did after a few deep breaths, and when I cracked my eyelids open, Tobias hadn't moved. He stood stoically beside that farmhouse sink.

The light from the window at his back limned his broad frame. His hair was longer than it had been our night together. The dark strands were slightly damp and finger-combed, like he'd come from the shower not long ago. Tobias's sculpted jaw was covered in a beard that went perfectly with the soft, buffalo-plaid flannel shirt molded to his muscled frame.

He looked like a sexy lumberjack.

"I like your beard."

He nodded. "So you've said."

Right. I'd told him that a few times six weeks ago, specifically when those bearded cheeks had been between my thighs.

That must have been before the condom broke and his sperm had freestyled through my vagina and into my fallopian tubes where one of them had dominated an egg.

Fucking sperm.

But hey, this could be worse. Tobias Holiday was a catch. He laughed often. His smile was as dazzling as the stars on a clear Montana night. Those blue eyes were like jewels, and they always shined especially bright when he was looking at me.

Or . . . they had once.

Now he was looking at me like I'd lost my mind.

Nope, just my menstrual cycle.

Speak, Eva. Say something. Anything. "Merry Christmas Eve."

"Merry Christmas Eve."

"Are you, um . . . doing anything?"

He nodded. "My parents' annual holiday party is tonight."

"On Christmas Eve?" I'd gone to that party many times but it had always been the week before Christmas.

"There was a scheduling conflict for last weekend."

"Ah. Well, that's always fun."

"Should be a good time."

I forced a shaky smile, then looked around the space, twisting to give him my back and hide the terror on my face.

Tobias's home was no doubt something he'd designed himself. It reminded me of one of the drawings he'd done in college. We'd gone on dates and he'd sketch houses on napkins while we'd waited for our food.

He'd always wanted a place in the country where he didn't have to worry about neighbors peering through his windows or the noise from constant traffic.

After years of bouncing from city to city, I'd probably go crazy out here alone.

"Eva." Tobias's deep voice had a slight rasp that always made my heart flip.

"Yes?" I stiffened.

"Will you turn around and look at me?"

I cringed but obeyed, turning just in time to see him push off the counter and come to the island, bracing his hands on the edge.

"What's wrong?"

"H-how do you know something is wrong?"

He shot me a flat look. "Eva."

It was unfair how well he knew me, even after all these years.

"I—" The sentence lodged in my throat.

"You're scaring me." The concern in his face broke my heart. "Is it your dad?"

I shook my head.

"Your sister?"

"No," I whispered. "It's . . ."

My hand tightened around the pregnancy stick so tightly, I worried it would crack. I closed my eyes again, squared my shoulders and did the first thing that came to mind.

I sang.

"On the third day of Christmas, my true love sent to me."

Tobias had always loved it in college when I'd make up stupid songs in the shower. He'd sneak into the bathroom and sit on the toilet to listen. He'd often scared the hell out of me when I'd pulled back the curtain and there he'd been, those blue eyes dancing at my ridiculous lyrics.

"Eva, what the hell is—"

I held up a finger. "Three French hens. Two turtle doves."

I opened my eyes, slid my hand out of my pocket and threw the stick at him.

Tobias snagged it from the air.

"And a partridge and a pregnancy."

CHAPTER TWO

TOBIAS

Think about it.

That's what Eva had told me two days ago after she'd thrown me that positive pregnancy test.

Think about it.

I'd done little else but think about it.

Eva was pregnant. We were having a baby. Holy fucking shit. Maybe we were having a baby. I'd been so stunned that I hadn't asked what she was planning. When we'd hooked up weeks ago, she'd told me her next move was to London. Was she still going?

The questions came like rapid fire. Did she want the baby? Did I?

Yes.

As I stared across the empty lobby at Holiday Homes, looking around the building I'd designed, *yes* might as well have been painted on the wall.

Yes, I wanted this baby. I wasn't prepared for it. I doubted Eva was either. But in my heart, the answer was yes. That was about the only conclusion I'd landed on in the past two days.

That, and I needed to talk to Eva.

I pulled my phone from my pocket, my heart beating like a bass drum in my chest as I found her number. It had been saved in my phone for years, but since our breakup in college, I'd called it only once.

After her father's stroke.

When my finger hit call, I leaned against the lobby's counter, afraid I might fall over if I wasn't propped up against something.

She answered on the third ring. "Hi."

"Hey."

Awkward silence dragged and dragged, but my heart just kept on thumping.

"How was your Christmas?" she asked.

"Fine. Yours?"

"It was nice. Just Dad and me hanging out. My sister and her husband and kids went to her in-laws."

"How is your dad?"

"He's good. The assisted living place he's in is really nice. He's got his own apartment and a bunch of friends."

"That's good."

"I never thanked you for the flowers you sent after his stroke. They were beautiful. Thank you."

"You're welcome." This small talk was as excruciating

as the nail I'd once accidentally driven into my hand with a nail gun. "We need to talk."

"Yeah." She sighed. "We do."

Even with the distraction of Christmas yesterday, the unanswered questions were beginning to fester. "Can you come over later?"

"Sure. What time?"

"I've got a meeting now for about an hour or two. Then I'll be heading home." The office was closed all week until after New Year's Day.

"I'll come over around two."

"See you then." I ended the call, tucked my phone away and some of the tightness in my chest loosened. Two o'clock. I only had to make it until two.

The front door opened and my brother Maddox strode into the building, drawing in a long breath. "Hey. Smells like Dad's old office in here."

"Brand-new building and it smells like the old one. But I like that." Like strong coffee and sawdust. That scent was the reason I'd spent my fair share of time in the office in the past two days. It grounded me. It was a constant when the world felt like it was spinning too fast in the wrong direction.

"Me too." Maddox walked over and shook my hand. "Thanks for meeting today."

It was me who was grateful. It would do me well to work. To pinch my fingers around a pencil and simply draw.

Maddox had decided to move home to Bozeman with his seven-year-old daughter, Violet. He'd been in California for years building his billion-dollar streaming company, Madcast. But his ex was a piece of work and escaping her by coming home held a lot of appeal.

Except he needed a home. Literally. And that's where I came in.

I was the chief architect at Holiday Homes and custom builds were our specialty. Our father had started this company out of the garage of my childhood home. He'd forsaken a parking place so he could store his tools inside. After decades of building quality houses around the Gallatin Valley, his reputation was unmatched.

Maddox had never taken an interest in construction or our mother's real estate company. He'd blazed his own trail. I'd always admired that about him. Maddox took risks. And damn, but they'd paid off.

Meanwhile my twin brother, Heath, and I had both landed here. We'd always loved tagging along with Dad to builds, and helping him organize tools in the garage or construct our own playhouses. Being at Holiday Homes fit, for us both.

Heath preferred management while I simply wanted to design beautiful buildings.

Maddox's house would definitely be in that category. He had the money for something magnificent, and I wouldn't let him down. Dad wasn't the only Holiday with a reputation to uphold. I was making a name for myself too.

"Want some coffee?" I asked, leading him toward the break room.

"Sure." He followed, taking in the office as we walked.

It was only three years old and ranked as one of my favorite projects. The beams I'd found for the vaulted ceilings had come from an old barn on a local ranch. I'd loved the hickory flooring so much I'd picked the same for my home. From the enormous gleaming windows to the wood-sided exterior, there wasn't a thing I'd change about this building.

"This is nice," Maddox said.

"You know Mom and Dad." They knew the value of beautiful buildings and didn't mind spending some money.

They'd worked hard their entire lives to build a legacy for their sons. They'd far exceeded their own expectations and had declared a few years ago that they were going to reap the rewards. They'd earned it.

Mom and Dad's massive home in the mountain foothills was another favorite of my designs. They'd given me free rein to be creative so I'd designed a home that blended and complemented the landscape.

Mom's only request had been bedrooms. Lots and lots of bedrooms. One was for Violet. And the others for her future grandbabies.

I guess she could earmark another room soon.

For my baby.

The sweater I'd pulled on this morning squeezed around my ribs like a ratchet strap, making it hard to breathe as we each carried steaming coffee mugs to my office.

"You okay?" Maddox asked as I took a seat behind the desk.

"Yeah," I lied, rubbing my beard. "Great."

Maddox didn't buy it. He studied my face, much like he had yesterday during the Christmas festivities at our parents' place. Violet had been the center of attention, entertaining us all as she'd opened her gifts. I'd hoped with her as the focal point, no one would notice that I'd been busy *thinking about it*.

Guess not.

"Missed you at the party at The Baxter," he said.

"Yeah. Had something come up." Impending fatherhood had killed my desire for dancing and drinking.

"Tobias."

I swallowed the lump in my throat.

"What happened?" he asked.

"Nothing."

"Talk to me. I've been a shit older brother as of late. Give me the chance to make up for it."

Maddox and I hadn't talked much lately. He'd been busy in California. I'd been busy here. I was looking forward to connecting with him again. To skiing on the weekends or grabbing a beer downtown.

Maybe he could teach me how to change a diaper.

"Do you remember Eva?" I asked, staring blankly at the wall.

"I never met her, but yeah." He leaned forward in his chair, giving me his undivided attention.

"She came over the other morning. Christmas Eve."

"Okay. Are you getting back together or something?"

"No." I rubbed my hands over my face, then spoke the words I still couldn't believe. "She's pregnant."

"Oh." The absent *shit* in that sentence hung in the air.

"We hooked up a while back. The condom broke. She's pregnant. And she's moving to London." There. The truth was out. Now I wanted to get to work. So I picked up a pencil from the desk. "Let's go through what you want for your house."

"We can do this another day."

I slid a notebook under the graphite tip and waited. "No, today's good."

"Tob—"

"Five bedrooms? Or would you like six?"

Maddox sighed but didn't push. "Six. And one in the guesthouse."

"Bathrooms?"

After an hour discussing his home, me asking questions, Maddox answering, I had what I needed and was ready to get home in case Eva showed up early. "I'll get a preliminary draft sketched and bring it over within the week."

"Thank you." He nodded, and after I showed him to the door, I put on my coat and locked the office behind me.

I drove the familiar streets through town until I reached the country road that wound toward the mountains. My home was in the center of a six-acre plot I'd bought before land prices in the valley had boomed. Mom had seen the listing come through and she'd known how much I wanted to live out of town.

I'd owned the land for two years before I'd broken ground on my own home. Now that it was complete, I couldn't imagine living anywhere else. Not only because this was another favorite build, but because Montana was home.

At least Eva was from here. That gave us one less hurdle to clear. Her family was here and it was the obvious place for us to raise this kid.

I pulled into the garage, heading inside, where I hovered in the living room, my gaze alternating between the floor and the windows that overlooked the driveway. The clock on the wall ticked too slowly, and every time I glanced up, expecting it to be nearly two, the hands had barely moved.

Its ticking grew louder and louder until I let out a frustrated groan and forced myself away from the living room. I stalked to my room, not for any particular reason just that its windows didn't face the front of the house. My feet stuttered to a stop when my gaze landed on the bed.

For weeks I'd pictured Eva there. Her dark hair spread

out on my pillow. Her hazel eyes locked with mine as I'd moved inside her.

I hadn't noticed the condom had broken. Granted, we'd had a bottle of wine downtown and another when we'd come here. By the time I'd given her three orgasms, I'd been spent and hadn't paid much attention.

Or maybe she'd scrambled my brain. Because that night with Eva, well . . . it had been like traveling back in time.

I walked to the dresser against the wall, easing open the top drawer. Buried beneath rows of folded socks, stuffed in the far corner next to my boxer briefs, was a square velvet box. The last time I'd held it in my hand was the day I'd moved in.

The hinges gave a small pop as I pushed open the top. A golden band sat firmly in the white satin enclosure. The marquise-cut solitaire diamond glinted under the bedroom light, like a star caught in this tiny box.

There was no logical reason for me to keep this ring. I'd bought it for Eva, and it wasn't like I was saving it for another woman.

Yet the day I'd taken it to the pawnshop, a broken-hearted twenty-two-year-old man, I hadn't been able to let it go. I'd walked to the counter, showed the shop's clerk the ring, and before he'd even muttered a price, I'd told him it was a mistake and walked out the door.

No one knew I'd proposed. Not my parents. Not my brothers.

I doubted Eva had told many people either. Maybe her father. Maybe not. I suspected she'd done much like I'd done and had tried to forget that night.

We'd dated through college. Eva and I had met in the dorm's cafeteria our freshman year, and after our first date —dinner at a pizza place and a movie—we'd been inseparable.

She'd mentioned wanting to move to a city and explore the world after graduation, but they'd always been offhand comments. Like dreams you threw into the air like a balloon, knowing it would catch the wind and vanish.

During our last semester, she'd applied at a few places in Bozeman. I hadn't realized those had been her backups, not her first choice.

She'd hidden a lot from me our senior year.

Like her plans to leave Montana. Like her plans to leave me. Like the interviews she'd had with a global construction company that specialized in managing large-scale projects. They helped build enormous, boxy, boring buildings around the world.

She'd kept it all quiet until I'd proposed.

After graduation, I'd taken her to a fancy dinner before bringing her to my apartment where I'd dropped down on one knee and asked her to be my wife. She'd taken one look at that ring and the truth had spilled out.

A life in Bozeman hadn't been her dream.

She'd left my apartment with tears streaming down her face, and seven days later, moved to New York.

We'd gone years without speaking. Mutual friends would give me random updates on her whereabouts. New York. San Francisco. Tokyo. Melbourne. Boston. Eva always seemed to be somewhere new.

Meanwhile, I'd been in Montana, wondering how many years it would take for me to let her go.

I hadn't realized until our night together six weeks ago that the resentment had faded. That instead of feeling angry toward her, I'd just . . . missed her.

Her laugh. Her snark. Her intelligence.

Her quirks. Her smile.

Our hookup had been for closure. Our second chance at a decent goodbye.

Now we were having a baby. Maybe. God, this was messed up.

I stuffed the ring into the drawer, shoving it closed, then crossed the bedroom as the sound of a car door slammed. I quickened my steps through the living room.

Would I find her on the sidewalk again? Or would she actually make it to the door? I'd learned a long time ago that rushing Eva usually meant she'd shut down. She needed a distraction whenever she was stuck, which was why I'd invented our thumb wars.

One of us always let the other win.

Today, I wouldn't give her thirty minutes in the cold. Freak-out or no. There'd be no thumb war. If I had to drag her inside, so be it. But when I opened the door, she was making her way up the sidewalk.

My sweater was too tight again, forcing my ribs together so I couldn't fill my lungs.

Eva's rich, chocolate hair was tied in a ponytail with a few tendrils framing her face. Her eyes were hidden behind a pair of mirrored sunglasses that reflected the bright white of the snow on my lawn. Her red parka was the same one she'd worn on Christmas Eve, but her hands weren't stuffed in her pockets this time.

She was beautiful. Always beautiful.

"Hi." I stepped aside, holding the door.

"Hi." She shoved the sunglasses into her hair as she stepped inside. Then she planted a hand against the wall to toe off her snowy boots. "How was work?"

"Fine. I was meeting with Maddox. He's moving home."

"Really? That's good. I'm sure your mom will love having all three of you in town."

"She will." The only thing Mom would have loved more would be for all of us to have wives so she could spoil her daughters-in-law. Especially had one of those been Eva.

I helped Eva from her coat, hanging it on a hook in the entryway, then waved her to the living room instead of the kitchen. Sitting on the couches seemed safer than the island. And considering her long-sleeved tee fit snugly to her body and her leggings left little to the imagination, I doubted she'd throw a stick coated in urine my way today.

"Your house is lovely." She ran her hand over the

leather arm of a chair. "The windows. The wood. The vaulted ceilings. The mountains outside to greet you good morning. The trees as neighbors to say good night. It's exactly what I would have expected you to build."

"Thanks."

That compliment seemed to diffuse a fraction of the tension in my spine. Like she knew I needed a millisecond of normal conversation. We might not have spoken much in recent years, but she knew me. And if there was a woman to go through this with, I wouldn't want it to be anyone else.

"So . . ." She plopped in the chair.

"You're pregnant."

"I'm pregnant." The words were hoarse and rough, like this was the first time she'd said them. Maybe it was. Eva met my gaze and there was an apology there. "About the other day. I didn't handle it very well."

"It's okay." No one but Eva would have made up fake lyrics to a Christmas carol to announce a pregnancy. Someday in the future, maybe that little jingle would make me laugh. Depending on what she did. "Have you decided what you're going to do?"

"It's not just my decision. We're sort of in this together."

"I appreciate that. But if it were just your decision, what would you want?"

She dropped her gaze to her lap. "I don't know if I'll be a good mother."

She would. Maybe she didn't have confidence in herself, especially given her own mother. But Eva would be a great mom.

Her heart was too full of love.

"You will be," I said.

She looked up to me with tears in her eyes. "I'd like the chance to try."

The air rushed from my lungs. "So would I."

I hadn't let myself hope for this answer but damn, it was good to hear. It didn't really lessen the panic or fear. But it gave us a direction.

A baby. We were having a baby.

"I didn't plan this, Tobias," she whispered. "To trick or trap you."

"The thought never crossed my mind." Maybe it would have if this were another woman, but not Eva.

"There's a lot to figure out. And not much time."

Wait. What? "What do you mean there's not much time? Don't we have eight or nine months?"

"Um . . . no."

It clicked, the conversation from weeks ago. Part of the reason we'd met was that she'd wanted to see me before she left Bozeman again. "Wait. You're still moving to London?"

"Yeah." She nodded. "My next job starts in a week."

A job in London.

Well . . . fuck.

CHAPTER THREE

EVA

Tobias. Was. Pissed.

On the outside, he looked exactly the same as he had seconds ago. Crystal-blue eyes. Attractive beard. A charcoal sweater that shouldn't have been sexy but was because it showcased his strong arms and broad shoulders.

It was his hands that gave him away. His hands always matched his mood.

His fingers dug into his thighs and the veins that traced up from his knuckles to his sinewed forearms were pulsing.

"It's only for six to eight months." *Or a year if we hit any delays, but I'd work extra hard to make sure it was done on time.*

"Six. To. Eight. Months?"

Oops. One-word enunciation wasn't a good sign.

Clearly explaining my job was not the right thing to say. "It, er . . . goes by fast."

Tobias blinked.

"London's not that far away." Just a teeny, tiny ocean. And most of the contiguous United States.

His nostrils flared. Those hands clamped tighter on his legs.

Shut up, Eva. I opened my mouth, but my brain engaged and clamped my lips together before more spewed out and I caused more damage.

"This changes everything." Tobias nodded to my belly. "Do I have a say in this?"

"In where I live? Well, no. I have a job. This is my career."

"How are we going to parent living on opposite sides of the globe?"

"Maybe we could rent Santa's sleigh?" I laughed.

Tobias did not. His hands balled into fists on the tops of his knees.

"I don't know, okay?" I tossed up my hands. "I don't know. I spent the past two days trying to wrap my head around the pregnancy. I haven't gotten to the actual child-rearing yet." I mean seriously, I was growing a human being. Wasn't I entitled to a week or so to process that one first?

"We need a plan," he declared.

Oh, how Tobias loved his plans. They were as dear to him as the first edition Millennium Falcon Lego set he'd had since middle school.

His talent for planning was what made him such a successful architect. His organizational skills and determination had made him a wealthy man, even at twenty-nine. But he clung to his plans like twinkle lights to a tree. Heaven forbid he give spontaneity a try.

Like move to New York with your girlfriend for one year. That was all I'd asked for. One year away from Montana, then we could assess. Make a new plan.

I'd loved him wholeheartedly, but I'd needed to spread my wings and see if they had the strength to fly.

Sure, Tobias had loved me too. Of that, I had no doubt. Maybe I hadn't loved him enough to give up my dreams. But he hadn't loved me enough to change his plans. He hadn't loved me enough to ask me to stay.

Why hadn't he asked me the night of the proposal to stay? I'd waited for it. I'd prepared a speech about the merits of living around other cultures and trying different experiences. Instead, he'd let me walk out the door.

And everything that I'd thought I'd known, everything I'd believed in—him, us—had been untethered. Shattered.

Turns out, I did know how to fly. I'd been flying on my own for years.

Our lives had split down different streams. Now we needed to find a way to merge them together again.

"We have time to figure this out. Months," I said. "Let's work together on a plan."

A statement I was sure would make him relax, but

instead, he shot off the couch and began pacing in front of his live-edge coffee table. His hands flexed and unflexed, over and over until I found myself copying the gesture too.

Gah! I tucked both beneath my legs.

"I don't want to miss the pregnancy, Eva."

"You don't?"

He stopped pacing and sent me a glare.

"Okay," I drawled. "Maybe you could fly out for some of the doctor's appointments. And we can FaceTime."

"FaceTime. You want me to be a father through FaceTime."

"I'm just throwing out options."

Tobias started pacing again. Back and forth. Back and forth. That poor, beautiful rug might not survive this pregnancy. "My life is here."

I'd heard that one before. "My job is not."

"This is bigger than your job."

Now it was my turn to get mad. "Then give up yours."

"You know I can't do that."

I opened my mouth but once more my brain engaged and stopped the stream of expletives before they could escape. This would only lead to the same stalemate we'd landed in years ago on the night he'd proposed.

We hadn't solved that puzzle then. I doubted we would today.

"I don't want to fight," I said.

"No, you just want to run away."

Ouch. "That's not fair."

"It's—sorry." His feet stopped. His shoulders fell. His hands relaxed. "I don't want to fight either."

I believed him. But I also believed that if I stayed here for much longer, we'd end up going twelve rounds, and I hated fighting with Tobias. "I'm in town for the whole week. Now that we know we're having this baby, let's think on it. We're intelligent adults. We can figure this out."

There was a lot more confidence in my voice than I felt. *Fake it until you make it.*

"All right." He nodded.

I stood from the couch and skirted the end table, stopping in front of him. Then I took his hands in mine and squeezed the last shreds of tension from his fingers. "I'm scared."

Tobias laced his fingers with mine. "Same."

"But if there's anyone I'd do this with, it's you."

His eyes softened. "Again, same."

"Call me later?"

"I will." He let me go and escorted me to the door, helping me into my coat. Then he stood on the stoop, waiting until I pulled away from his house before going inside.

When his house had disappeared from my rearview, I let out the breath I'd been holding.

Not bad. Not great, but not bad.

He wanted the baby. That was a good thing. A *great* thing. Kids needed dads, and I couldn't imagine life without my own. And Tobias would be a wonderful father.

We just had to figure out logistics, and luckily, he wasn't the only specialist in that area. Yes, this was a lot different than constructing a building, but we'd manage, especially if we didn't rush a decision.

There was time. I wasn't leaving until New Year's Day.

Traffic picked up as I reached the outskirts of town. Bozeman had grown considerably over the years since I'd been gone. As a kid, Dad would take my sister and me to Bozeman from our little town of Manhattan. The twenty-mile stretch between communities had been mostly prairie.

I'd driven out yesterday for nostalgia's sake, even though a new family lived in the home I'd once called mine. Where open fields of wheat and barley had bloomed a decade ago, housing developments had sprouted instead.

But despite the traffic and influx of residents, this valley was still home. A landing place for the holidays. For the past three months, I'd been fortunate to call it home.

My company had been contracted to oversee the development of a data center. Another project liaison had been tasked with the beginning of the project. I'd already been assigned to a job in Houston, otherwise, I would have vied for it. But the other woman had quit three months ago, and I'd managed to slide in and take her place.

Turnover was fairly constant. Though my job paid

well, it was demanding. Sometimes I'd see a project from start to finish. Other times, I'd be pulled to smooth the feathers of a frazzled client.

London was one of those jobs. The client was temperamental and didn't like the current project manager. Enter Eva.

I'd be a fresh face for them to chastise. Or maybe I'd win them over.

Next week, I'd know which way this one was going to go.

But for now, I was savoring my last days in Montana.

Three months here had given me long-overdue time with my dad. I'd been able to spend evenings at Elena's home, getting to know her two daughters.

And Tobias.

During my first month here, I'd worried about seeing him. If I wasn't at the jobsite, Dad's home or Elena's place, I'd basically existed as a recluse. Mostly out of fear that he hated me. But partly at the idea of seeing him with another woman on his arm.

Then I'd bumped into his mom at the grocery store. Hannah had been so happy to see me that she'd pulled me into her arms with tears swimming in her eyes. I'd had them in mine too. Hannah Holiday was arguably the best woman I'd ever known. We'd stood in the frozen foods section for so long that the ice cream in my cart had melted.

She'd hinted that Tobias was single and had encouraged me to reach out. It had taken me days to work up the nerve. But one evening after a bottle of cabernet for bravery, I'd called the same number I'd memorized years ago and invited him to meet for a drink.

When I'd walked into the bar that night six weeks ago, he'd hugged me. And we'd just . . . clicked.

It was the reason I knew we could do this. He could still have his life here. I could have mine, and together, we'd have this baby.

"We can do this." My reassurance rushed over the steering wheel. We could do this.

The condo my company had found for me was next to a golf course, the greens and fairways hidden by a blanket of pristine snow. The bare aspen and cottonwood trees were covered in ice, their branches glittering with crystals that caught the sun in the cloudless blue sky.

Bozeman was sunny, even in winter. I'd miss the constant sunshine when in London. The few times I'd visited, it had rained and rained.

There was a U-Haul moving truck in the driveway to the condo beside mine. As I parked and made my way to the front door, a man came out carrying a box. He waved, pausing like he was going to introduce himself. I simply waved and disappeared inside.

There was no point in introducing myself. I'd be gone before he unpacked.

It was cold inside the condo, or maybe it just seemed cold because it was empty. I dropped my purse and keys on the floor in the living room, then kicked off my shoes before walking to the one piece of furniture that hadn't been shipped to England or sold online.

An air mattress.

It was pushed against the living room wall. The sleeping bag I'd bought was laid neatly on top. I'd decided to sleep here instead of in the bedroom because the gas fireplace kept this room cozy at night.

I plopped down on the mattress and grabbed my laptop from the floor, propping it on my lap as I leaned against the pillow. The data center was done, only waiting on the cleaning crew, and most people had taken this week off for the holidays. My inbox was mostly empty. With nothing to do at night but stare at the place where the TV had been, I'd resorted to working. Which wasn't all that different than when the TV had been here.

My job was my best friend. And I loved her. Most days.

Today, I was a little lonely. This feeling usually came when I was wrapping up one project and gearing up for the next.

The barren rooms didn't help. The movers had already come to clear out this condo. What I hadn't wanted to ship, I'd sold on Facebook and Craigslist. Sure, I could just buy new furniture or lease a furnished home, but I had this thing about my own stuff. Especially my own bed.

My boss indulged the added expense, mostly because I

never balked when he asked me to move. So my bed went with me everywhere. At the moment, it was being set up in my London apartment, hence the air mattress.

My suitcase in the bathroom had enough clothes and toiletries to last me the week. I'd pack it up too and board a plane on Sunday. Six days.

Then I wouldn't have time to be lonely.

The London project was a fulfillment center for an online retailer. They were building a new warehouse outside the city, and given the most recent status update, it was proving to be a challenge.

Tobias would probably scoff if I told him that a square building made mostly of steel and concrete could be so complex. It was exactly the type of structure he'd loathe.

He'd already given me a ration of shit for helping on the data center *monstrosity* we'd built outside Bozeman. He wasn't entirely wrong. The blocked walls did contrast sharply with the beautiful mountain landscape.

But aside from its lack of character, the center was done and now it was time for me to move along. I'd harass foremen and argue with suppliers until another ugly building was marring a different landscape.

The nature of my job meant I didn't have a cushy office. I usually had a desk in a dirty construction trailer staged beside the portable toilets. Certainly no place for a baby.

I pressed my hand to my belly.

How was this going to work? My job was demanding.

Twelve hours was a short day. I was usually the first to arrive on site and the last to leave. My boss liked having us hover close to each build, but maybe he'd be okay with me working from home a few days a week.

I'd have to hire a nanny. There was no question. It wasn't like I'd have friends to babysit or pitch in. I never stayed long enough in one city to make reliable friends.

That hadn't bothered me until today.

Who would I call in an emergency? Could I find a nanny who'd be willing to work the nights when I'd have dinner with clients? How often would we be able to get away and visit Tobias?

I couldn't expect him to come to us every month. I took three, maybe four vacation days a year. The London project was behind schedule, and once I started, it would be a dead sprint to the finish line.

Unless . . . oh, God. What if he wanted full custody? What if I was the parent doing the visitation?

No. Tobias would never do that to me. He had to know that would break me apart.

He had to know I'd despise him for trying.

The questions and worries screamed at me in the empty space. The walls began closing in, so I climbed off the mattress and hurried toward the door. The car's seats were still warm as I drove away.

There were two places I went regularly, either my sister's or my dad's, and the sedan seemed to steer itself to my father's assisted living home. I parked in the same place I'd parked yesterday for Christmas, and walked inside the building, waving to the woman stationed at the reception desk. Dad called the receptionists his wardens because they kept track of when he left and when he came home.

Not that he left often. Most of his friends from my youth still lived in Manhattan. And the friends he'd made since moving here all lived close so he'd simply visit them in their respective apartments.

The home provided grocery deliveries and had a dining room, serving three meals per day. On occasion, my sister would take Dad to her house so he could play with the girls. But mostly, she'd bring her daughters here because Dad preferred it that way.

He'd confessed to me yesterday that he often felt like a burden on Elena.

I'd confessed to him yesterday that I often felt like I'd abandoned them both.

But it was my job that paid for this home. Elena was a stay-at-home mom with two kids, living off her husband's single income. She couldn't afford this facility. Dad hadn't wanted an in-home nurse, and in another one of his confessions, he'd told me that the house reminded him too much of Mom.

He was happy in his apartment. Therefore, I'd happily pay so he had help close by if necessary.

Dad's door was open as I walked down the hallway. The television was blaring.

I smirked before knocking loudly so he'd hear me over the noise.

"It's loud enough, Nancy!" He shuffled out of the kitchen, his bad side leaning heavily into a cane. "Eva?"

"Hi, Daddy."

"What did you say?"

I rolled my eyes and pointed to the television.

"Oh." With his good hand, he reached into his jeans pocket and pulled out the remote, hitting the power button.

Blissful silence flooded the room.

"Eddy, I can't hear it!" Nancy shouted from across the hall.

I pulled in my lips to hide my smile as I closed the door. "I see that Nancy still hasn't gotten her television fixed."

"No." He grumbled something under his breath as he made his way to his recliner. "There's a chance I'll go deaf if she doesn't get it replaced soon."

Nancy had been Dad's neighbor since he'd moved in. She was twenty years his senior and he treated her like a beloved grandparent. Her television wasn't just old and outdated, the volume hadn't worked in weeks. Rather than cross the hallway to watch Dad's TV, Nancy preferred to watch from her own apartment so she could sit in her own chair. For the past month, she'd pick a channel and Dad would crank the volume on his so she could hear.

"What are you up to? Figured you'd be at work." He pulled the lever to raise the footrest on his chair.

"No, today's been quiet." I unzipped my coat and tugged it off before plopping onto his overstuffed loveseat. "How are you feeling?"

He gave me a crooked smile. "Right as rain."

Dad was the youngest resident at this home by decades. Three years ago, he'd suffered a massive, fluke stroke. He struggled with movement and function with the left side of his body. For a few terrifying days, we hadn't known if he'd survive it. But he'd come a long way, thanks to extensive speech, physical and occupational therapies.

His words were still slurred and there were movements that would always cause him trouble, but he was alive. That was all I cared about.

This assisted living facility had been my idea after he'd rejected the idea of an in-home nurse. It was more like apartments than a nursing home and Dad had trained caregivers on hand in case of an emergency.

I hoped every day there wasn't one. Because the guilt from being halfway across the country when he'd had his stroke plagued me daily.

Guilt was about to become a constant companion again. It always hit hard after a visit home, and having been here for so long this time, I was sure the feeling would linger. Especially when I tossed Tobias and the baby into the mix.

"You okay?" Dad asked.

"Great." I forced a bright smile. "Just wanted to stop in and say hi. It's pretty quiet at my place."

"Want to watch something?" He waved the remote.

"Sure." I tucked my legs under me and relaxed into the couch, as Dad found us a sitcom rerun.

I stayed for two episodes, then kissed Dad's cheek goodbye because he'd fallen asleep.

It was getting dark as I drove home, the winter days short and cold. I shivered behind the wheel, wishing I had more work to do this week. Idle time was dangerous to my mental health. I didn't want to think about how my life mirrored my mother's more than my father's.

Traveling and bouncing from address to address hadn't been a problem a week ago. But then I'd taken that pregnancy test and now . . . everything was different.

My street was quiet. The moving truck was gone— maybe they'd finished unloading. The neighbors' homes were all aglow. Only my condo sat dark and empty.

Except it wasn't exactly empty. There was a truck in the driveway, parked beside my space.

My heart did a little flip.

It always flipped for Tobias.

I wasn't sure why he was here, waiting on my porch. But it was nice to come home and not be alone.

CHAPTER FOUR

TOBIAS

Eva led the way inside her condo. I'd expected furniture. Maybe a houseplant. Maybe boxes. Instead, the space was empty save for an air mattress in the living room next to the gas fireplace.

"Where's your stuff?" I asked as she flipped on the lights.

"Most of it's in London. The couch and a few other furniture items were sold because the flat I'm renting isn't all that big."

"How long has it all been gone?"

She shrugged and unzipped her coat. "Two weeks?"

I blinked. She'd been sleeping on an air mattress for two weeks with one more to go. "Why didn't your company put you up in a hotel?"

"I didn't ask. And I don't mind the air mattress."

That was a lie. Eva's voice was too bright. This woman

loved a comfortable bed. In college, she'd insisted we stay at her place most nights because her pillow-top mattress had been softer than mine.

The idea of her sleeping on the floor, living like a transient, set my teeth on edge. She couldn't stay here. Not like this.

"You should stay in my guest bedroom this week." The offer flew out of my mouth, but I didn't hate it. In fact, it wasn't a horrible idea. "That will give us a chance to talk. And the mattress in my guest bedroom is a good one."

"No, that's okay. I don't want to put you out."

"It's a memory foam."

She glanced at the air mattress and grimaced. "I like memory foam."

"Go pack. I insist."

"I forgot how stubborn you are."

"No, you didn't." I chuckled. "You just forgot that you liked it."

She rolled her eyes. "You have me mistaken for one of your other ex-girlfriends."

Never. There was no mistaking Eva for any other woman. Not that there'd been many. The only woman I'd spent time with lately was Chelsea, and our casual hookups when she was passing through town were far from serious. And I hadn't seen her in months.

"What's it gonna be, Williams? Air mattress or memory foam?"

"Fine. You win. I'll take your guest bed," she said,

nodding to her setup on the floor. "But only because that thing has a slow leak and my back is starting to hurt."

"Would you like me to roll that up while you get your stuff?"

"Tonight?"

I shrugged. "Might as well."

"Okay. I'll get its case."

She scurried away and I toed off my shoes so I wouldn't drag snow clumps over the hardwood floors. Then I started with the sleeping bag. The scent of Eva's favorite vanilla bean lotion caught my nose as I folded it into a tight roll.

After our breakup, I'd found a bottle of that lotion in my bathroom. It had taken me a year to toss it out. Then our night together six weeks ago, I'd caught that scent and the next words out of my mouth had been an invitation.

Come home with me.

I hadn't asked. Just another insistence.

And after we'd fucked the first time, against a wall because neither of us had been able to wait, I'd carried her to my bed where I'd let that scent soak into my sheets.

Christ, one whiff and I was hard. A cold shower would be in order when I got home. With a clenched jaw, I tied the straps on the bundled sleeping bag.

Eva came out and tossed me the case for the air mattress, and less than five minutes later, she rolled out a suitcase. "Want some help?"

"No, I've got this." The last of the air was rushing out

of the mattress's vent as I folded it into sections. "Just grab the rest of your stuff."

"Oh, this is it."

A single suitcase and a backpack over her shoulder. That grated as hard as the empty apartment. The Eva I'd known hadn't gone anywhere without a bagful of books and a purse so large it could double as a pillowcase.

"Why are you looking at me like that?" she asked.

"Is this what your life has been like? Empty apartment to empty apartment?"

"It's only empty because I'm in transition."

"How often do you transition?"

"Depends." She lifted a shoulder. "Once or twice a year. Sometimes more. Sometimes less."

So she'd spend one or two months a year living with barren walls and a handful of wardrobe pieces. Why did she even bother unpacking? Did this air mattress go with her? Or did she just buy a new one at every transition?

This lifestyle of hers sank into my skin like a rash. This wasn't what I wanted for her. But I guess that didn't matter. This was the life she'd wanted for herself. I'd learned years ago that I had no say.

But where this baby was concerned . . . something had to give.

"I don't mind, Tobias," she said as I began to shove the folded mattress into the case. "I'm not home much while I'm on a project."

"Home?" There was a snark to my voice.

Eva's eyes narrowed. "Home can have different meanings to different people. To me, it's not four walls. It's not a piece of land or a town or a state."

"Then where is home?"

"I guess . . . I've carried it with me." She pressed a hand to her heart. "That's enough for me."

"Except it isn't just you anymore."

Eva raised her chin. "You act like I'm homeless. I'm moving. People move for their jobs. My job means that I can pay for my dad's home. And I *like* my job. Why is that so wrong?"

"It's not. Let's . . . forget it." I sighed, then finished packing up the air mattress, carrying it, her sleeping bag and pillow to the door. "I'm just trying to wrap my head around this, Eva."

"So am I." She gave me a sad smile. "We can figure out the logistics. But maybe me coming to stay is a bad idea. I can get a hotel."

"No." I shook my head. If I actually thought she'd go to a hotel, I might let this go. But she was just as stubborn as I was, and after I left, she'd unroll this air mattress. "Stay with me. Please."

"Only because you have the memory foam."

"And more than one pillow." I laughed and picked up her suitcase. Pillows, she'd once told me, were as important as the mattress.

"Now you're just bragging," she teased.

"Lead the way." I managed to carry everything in one

trip to my truck, then waited for her to lock up her condo before we headed across town and down the quiet roads to my house.

Home.

Wasn't a home a place where you could escape? Where you could find peace? Maybe she didn't need four walls to feel at home, but as I pulled into my garage, weight left my shoulders.

It was the reason I'd become an architect. Designing houses wasn't simply making them aesthetically pleasing. It was about creating a sanctuary. It was about giving others the foundation where they could grow roots that ran as deeply as my own.

I hit the button to the second stall and climbed out, waving Eva inside. When her car was parked, I retrieved her suitcase and hauled it inside. "Are you hungry?"

"Sure." She shrugged. "I'm an expert on takeout. Want me to order us something?"

"Or I can cook."

"You're letting me stay. I'll get dinner tonight."

"Okay." I nodded and watched as she scrolled through her phone, her fingers flying over the screen.

She didn't ask what I wanted to eat. She didn't have to.

Eva knew I hated chili. She knew I preferred cooked vegetables to raw. She knew that I drank water with every meal and that I kept homemade buttermilk ranch in the fridge because I always picked it over ketchup.

She knew me, better than anyone.

47

I'd missed the familiarity and how easy it was to be around her.

"Want something to drink?" I asked, opening the fridge.

"Water's fine."

I filled two glasses, mine with ice and hers without because it bothered her teeth. Then we settled in the living room on opposite ends of the couch. "It feels like days, not hours, since you came over."

She laughed, tucking her legs beneath her in the cushion. "I was just thinking that same thing."

Next to her on an end table was a digital frame. Eva picked it up, watching as the photos changed.

"Mom gave me that for Christmas yesterday." I watched past her shoulder, waiting until . . .

Eva gasped. "She put one of us in here?"

It was a photo Mom had taken years ago. One she'd had framed in her office for a few years. I suspected it was still in a drawer, tucked away for safekeeping. Mom had never given up hope that Eva would find her way home.

In the picture, Eva and I were lying on the couch in Mom and Dad's old house. I was asleep on my stomach, wearing only a pair of shorts. Eva was asleep on my naked back. My mouth was open. Her hair was spread over my shoulders and a strand had stuck to her lips.

It shouldn't have been comfortable, but I'd lost track of the times we'd slept like that. Totally content as long as we had each other.

"We look so . . . young." A smile lit up her face, but like the photo, it was gone too soon.

The next shot was of Heath and me on the ski hill a few winters ago. It was a selfie he'd insisted on taking on the chair lift. The next was a picture from last year's Christmas party. I stood beside Dad, each of us with a tumbler of whisky in our hands.

Eva and I watched the pictures rotate the full loop until the one of us returned. She ran her finger across the frame.

A flash of headlights forced us both from the couch. She set down the frame as I went to the door to meet the delivery driver.

"Burritos?" I asked, peeking inside the bag. "You don't like burritos."

"Actually, I do like them." She took a seat at the island, unwrapping the foil from her dinner while I sat beside her and did the same.

"Since when?"

"I lived in San Antonio for about five months. Around the corner from my rental was this burrito place. One night I got home late from work and there was nothing in the fridge. I didn't want to wait for pizza so I decided one burrito wouldn't kill me."

I laughed. "Obviously it didn't."

"I got it with queso. Now . . ." She lifted her burrito and took a huge bite, moaning as she chewed. "I love queso."

It was erotic, watching her eyes fall shut. There was a drop of melted cheese on the corner of her mouth. I lifted a hand, ready to wipe it away, then remembered that she was no longer mine. So I slid a napkin over and focused on my own meal.

When the wrappers were wadded up and tossed in the trash, Eva yawned. "I think I'm going to crash."

"I'll show you to your room." I collected her suitcase from the mudroom, then headed to the opposite end of the house, in the bedroom farthest from my own.

It seemed safer to put the bulk of my four-thousand square feet between us.

"Thanks for this," she said as I set the suitcase down inside the door.

"No problem. Can I get you anything?"

"This looks perfect." She glanced around the room, her eyes landing on the bed.

The comforter was a shade of deep green, much like the flecks in her hazel eyes. The sleigh-style frame was a rich brown close to the color of her hair. And if I stripped her out of those clothes, her skin would be the same alabaster as the walls.

We'd been together so many times it was like second nature to picture her on the bed. I could hear the hitch in her breath when I pushed inside her body. I could taste the sweetness of her tongue. I could feel her orgasm pulsing around my flesh. One inhale of her vanilla scent and my cock twitched.

Shit. I had to get the fuck out of this room and far away from this, or any, bed. "I'll let you get some sleep."

But before I could head to my primary suite for that cold shower, Eva's hand shot out, her fingers wrapping around my elbow. "Tobias?"

"Yeah?" My gaze fixed on her mouth.

"Good night." She stepped closer, wrapping her arms around my waist.

My arms encircled her immediately, pulling her close and burying my nose in her hair. Holding her was another automatic instinct.

I'd missed the way she fit against my frame. I'd missed her long hair threaded through my fingers. I'd missed the softness of her breasts and the tickle of her breath against my neck.

She sighed, sinking into my embrace. Then she leaned away, her eyes traveling up my neck and landing on my lips. Her mouth parted.

And that was the moment my resolve shattered.

I swept in, framed her face with my hands and sealed my mouth over hers. One sweep of my tongue across her bottom lip and she opened on a whimper.

Eva clung to me, her fingertips digging into my biceps as she rose up on her toes.

I slanted my mouth over hers, our tongues twisting in a kiss that should have been familiar. We'd kissed hundreds of times. Maybe thousands.

But there was desperation to this kiss. Even more

desperation than had been there our night weeks ago. Every anxiety about what was to come, every worry and doubt, we poured into the moment.

I ached for her, and when my arousal dug into her hip, she pressed in deeper, the urgency growing. Until I reached between us, intending to flip the button on her jeans, but froze when my knuckles grazed her belly.

Eva tensed, her lips still pressed to mine.

This wasn't a reckless trip down memory lane. This wasn't two former lovers enjoying a night of passion. This wasn't a man and woman giving in to an urge.

This wasn't just about us anymore.

I tore my mouth away and took a step back, dragging a hand over my beard as I worked to regain my breath. "Sorry."

"Me too." She walked to the corner of the bed and put five feet between us.

"Night." I stalked out of the room, pulling the door closed behind me. Then I jogged down the hallway, heading straight for my own bedroom.

My blood was on fire. My heart raced. I closed myself in the bathroom and turned on the shower. "Fuck."

What were we doing? What was I doing?

Those questions ran over and over in my head as I stepped beneath the cold spray. Water streamed down my skin. A trickle ran down the bridge of my nose as my hand found my shaft and stroked. The release was quick and unsatisfying. My body craved hers, not my fist.

I wasn't sure how long I stayed in the shower. Long enough to cool down. Then I toweled off and stepped in front of the mirror.

What am I doing?

Eva wasn't going to give up her job. She'd made that perfectly clear. She'd also admitted today that she didn't have a home.

Kids needed homes. They needed a resting place. They needed roots and routine.

I had all of those in spades.

Which meant if she didn't change her mind, I wouldn't have a choice. Once this baby was born, he or she was coming home to Montana.

I stared at my reflection, hating myself so much that I couldn't hold my own gaze.

If Eva was going to fight for London and the next move and the next move, then I'd fight her for my child. And she'd hate me. She'd fucking hate me.

But my kid was worth the fight.

And I'd just drawn the battle lines with a kiss.

CHAPTER FIVE

EVA

The scent of sausage links and syrup greeted me when I emerged from the bedroom.

I tiptoed down the hallway, hovering at its mouth, and watched as Tobias moved around his kitchen.

The smell held a memory that transported me straight into the past.

I was eighteen again, walking in a cafeteria with a blue plastic tray in my hands. Surrounded by a mass of other freshmen at Montana State all craving breakfast on a Saturday to chase away their Friday-night hangovers, I met the boy who'd won my heart.

All because of pancake syrup.

Tobias was no longer that boy. I was no longer that girl. But it was still impossible to tear my eyes away.

He shut off the stove, taking his spatula and lifting out the sausage to his plate. His broad shoulders were covered in a long-sleeved thermal, the red color making his hair look darker. I'd always liked it when he wore red, though not as much as blue, which brought out his eyes.

I kept my breaths short and low, not wanting him to catch me spying. A yawn tugged at my mouth but I kept my teeth clamped. Sleep had been elusive last night. Even on one of the most comfortable beds I'd slept on in years, I hadn't been able to shut off my brain.

Instead, I'd replayed that kiss.

That desperate, reckless, incredible kiss.

Staying here under his roof was probably a huge mistake. Temptation was going to run rampant. But at least it was just for a week.

Tobias pulled out a bottle of Log Cabin, squeezing a puddle next to his links.

"Still forgetting your pancakes with that syrup," I said, pushing off the wall.

He chuckled, glancing over his shoulder. "I made scrambled eggs. There's a brand-new bottle of ketchup in the fridge so you can ruin them."

I smiled and strode into the kitchen, taking a seat at the island.

He came and sat down, not at the stool beside mine, but one apart. He kept that boundary, then cut a piece of sausage and swirled it in syrup.

"Whenever I smell syrup, I think of the day we met," I said.

"The day you called me a monster." There was a smirk on his mouth as he chewed.

"Hey, the truth hurts, baby."

I'd come into the cafeteria, still in the sweatpants I'd worn to bed the previous night. My hair had been a wreck. Not a smidge of makeup had been left on my face except for the mascara smudges under my eyes. It had been the second month of freshman year and the first time I'd ever dared leave my dorm room not looking perfect.

But my hangover had been punishing. I'd been desperate for fluffy carbs to cure my headache. I'd heaped a pile of pancakes on my plate, but when I'd gone to smother them with syrup, Tobias had been at the dispenser, pumping the last few drops onto his sausage links.

"You made up a song," he said, forking another bite. "Remember it?"

I'd made up a bunch of stupid songs over the years, taking popular songs and replacing their lyrics with my own nonsense. Most of them I forgot the moment I was done with my rendition. But that one I remembered.

"Hello, can you hear me?" I sung, crooning Adele's song. "I'm in the cafeteria, dreaming about maple syrup and whipped cream."

Tobias shook his head, a smile on his perfect mouth. "Whenever the real song comes on the radio, I laugh."

"Me too," I lied.

The truth was, that song usually made me sad.

Because that song was Tobias's song. There I'd been, hungover and smelly and distraught over my lack of syrup, and Tobias had righted my day. He'd stolen the tray from my hands, taken it to a nearby table and spooned syrup onto my pancakes.

When he'd returned me my tray, I'd let out a pitiful whimper, then told him I loved him.

He'd sat beside me during that breakfast, and after I'd inhaled my pancakes, he'd asked me on a date.

That same night, he'd picked me up from my dorm room. Dinner. Movie. A typical date for two college kids. Then he'd walked me to my door and kissed me good night.

But nothing about that kiss had been typical. Because after that date, we hadn't spent a day apart. Not until the breakup.

We'd been inseparable. Insatiable.

In love.

We'd tackled life together.

Until . . . we hadn't.

"Help yourself." Tobias nodded toward the stove. "Unless you're not feeling well."

"No, I'm okay. No morning sickness so far." I slid from my stool and picked up the empty plate he'd left for me. Then I scooped eggs and sausage onto my plate, stopping at the fridge for ketchup before resuming my seat.

We ate in silence.

We did not mention last night's kiss.

57

I could still feel his tongue against mine, insistent and firm. That man craved control in every way but especially in the bedroom. When the lights were off and our clothes on the floor, he'd always been the one in charge. He'd never disappointed.

Tobias was better than a vibrator with fresh batteries.

At eighteen, as an unsure girl with zero experience except for a few awkward make-out sessions my senior year in high school, Tobias had been a dream. He'd made me feel wanted. He'd taught me about my body and its desires. He'd given me the freedom to let my inhibitions go and simply feel.

We'd been together countless times, each better than the last. Tobias always seemed to learn new tricks.

Like last night's kiss. He'd fluttered his tongue against mine and I'd nearly come undone.

Maybe it was just the hormones. Maybe it was because it had been a while since I'd had an orgasm—the last courtesy of Tobias. He'd been my one and only.

I refused to think that another woman had taught him that tongue flutter.

Jealousy snaked up my spine as I squirted ketchup on my plate. Irrational, green jealousy.

It had been my choice to walk away. I couldn't exactly fault him for moving on. Still . . . it soured the food on my tongue.

"Is it okay?" he asked.

"Great." I took another bite.

Compartmentalization had become a welcome companion so I shoved away the idea of another woman in Tobias's bed.

This wasn't the time for jealousy. This was the time for eating.

I forked a bite of eggs and dunked it in ketchup. "This is delicious."

"Are you working today?" he asked, taking his plate to the sink while I devoured my meal.

"A little. I'll probably set up camp right here if you don't mind."

"Go for it."

"And you? Are you going into town?" *Say yes.*

"Yes."

I tried not to let my shoulders sag in relief.

If he stayed here, I wasn't sure what would happen. That stool between us would only stay empty for so long before one of us caved. He was just too . . . easy. Too mouthwatering.

"Our office is closed this week," he said. "But I've got more work than I can keep up with so I'll probably head in for a while. Give you some space."

Give *us* some space.

"Okay." I stood and took my empty plate to the kitchen, careful not to get too close as I rinsed it at the sink and put it in the dishwasher.

"Make yourself at home," he said, then plucked a small black remote from a drawer beside the fridge.

"Here's a spare garage remote so you can come and go as you need."

"Thank you." I took it, then took one step away.

He did the same, rubbing a hand over his beard. "About last night. Sorry."

"It was just a kiss, Tobias. It's not like we haven't kissed before, right?"

"Yeah." His eyes locked with mine, his expression unreadable. Before I could make any sense of it, he strode from the room. Then the garage door opened and he was gone.

Why had he kissed me? Why did it look like he regretted it?

"Ugh." I wrapped my arms around my waist as my stomach twisted.

Maybe it was the hormones, maybe it was the stress of the unknown, maybe it was my ketchup, but I rushed to the bathroom as the wave of nausea crashed into me like a tsunami.

"So much for my eggs," I groaned as I emerged from a solid thirty minutes of hugging the toilet.

I swiped my phone from the nightstand and retreated to the living room couch, lying on my back as I scrolled through emails. I was typing out a reply to my boss when it rang. My mother's name flashed across the screen.

"Hi, Mom," I answered, forcing cheer into my voice.

"Hi, Eva." There was a bustle of noise behind her and

a woman speaking over an intercom. It was the typical soundtrack to Mom's calls.

"Where are you?"

"Atlanta, for about an hour. Then PDX." *Portland.*

Before I was in third grade, I'd been able to name every major city and its three-letter airport abbreviation. We'd had a map at home, and after every one of Mom's calls, I'd run to pinpoint where she was and where she was going, drawing imaginary lines between imaginary places.

Many of those cities weren't so imaginary now.

Mom was living in Miami. At least, she had been the last time we'd spoken. That had been four months ago on my birthday. She'd missed her regular Christmas call this week.

"I'm coming to Bozeman tomorrow. I just talked to Elena and she said you were there until after New Year's."

Shit. Thanks, Elena. "Um . . . yeah."

"We're all having dinner tomorrow." Not a question or an invitation, just a declaration.

"Okay." I'd planned to see Dad but I guess I'd go to his apartment for lunch instead.

"See you then." She hung up before I could say goodbye.

My stomach roiled again and I studied the ceiling until the sickness passed. Leave it to Tobias to have a tongue-and-groove painted ceiling, a shade lighter than the walls. No simple white ceilings here.

My phone rang again and I pressed it to my ear,

already knowing it was Elena. "Yes, she called me. Yes, I'll be over for dinner."

"Good." She sighed. "You have to be the buffer."

"'Kay." I'd been the buffer between Elena and Mom my entire life. "Want me to bring anything?"

"Wine."

Wine I wouldn't be drinking. "You got it. Anything else?"

"No. Can you believe she just calls and expects us to drop everything to accommodate her schedule?"

"That's Mom." It didn't annoy me like it annoyed Elena.

"I'm not telling Dad she's here."

"Fine by me." It would only upset him and Mom would be gone on the next flight out.

It was rare that she came to Montana. It was even rarer that she'd stay longer than twenty-four hours.

Mom was a pilot for a commercial airline. She'd earned her wings and nothing would keep her from the sky, not even a husband and two little girls. My entire life she'd traveled, leaving Dad to care for Elena and me.

The times when Mom took a vacation and would be home for an extended period were usually the nights when I'd wake to hear my parents fighting. It was her absence that had made their marriage last as long as it had.

If you could even call it a marriage. They'd made their divorce official after I'd graduated from high school, but they'd written off each other years before the papers had been signed.

Elena harbored a lot of bitterness toward Mom, mostly on Dad's behalf. He'd been a married, single parent. He'd shouldered all the laundry after a ten-hour workday. He'd cooked the meals and packed the lunches. He'd painted our nails and plaited braids into our hair.

Dad had been both father and mother.

Elena had wanted an actual mother, not because he'd failed in any way, but because girls needed moms.

Maybe the reason it hadn't bothered me the way it had her was because I'd known that Mom would have paled in comparison to Dad. He'd made up for her shortcomings ten times over.

And we'd been better, just the three of us.

My hand splayed across my flat belly. "We'll figure this out, won't we?"

There wasn't another choice. When I looked to my parents, the one I aspired to imitate was not my mother.

But her income had meant a mortgage-free home. It had meant college tuitions. On some of her longer stays, after the first day or two of awkwardness, we'd settle into a new routine. Mom would take us shopping and out to a girls' only lunch.

She hadn't been a bad parent. Just . . . absent.

Elena wanted her to change, something that would never happen. Part of the reason I suspected Elena didn't work was because she was so worried about showing any resemblance to Mom.

Elena's daughters would always have a parent at home. They'd have a mother dedicated to each and every aspect of their lives. Mom might be a pilot, but Elena would be the helicopter mother, hovering over the girls until they finally left home.

There had to be a middle ground. I could find a balance, right? Granted, I had no husband to help. That would make it more difficult. But in my heart of hearts, I knew I could find the middle ground. I could be successful like Mom in my career. I could be the mother this baby deserved.

The logistics of that eluded me at the moment, but there was time to plan this out. For now, I'd finish out my week.

I'd be the *buffer*, the peacekeeper, at dinner tomorrow, ensuring Mom and Elena didn't get into an argument. I'd fill the conversation with questions about Mom's recent trips and what her schedule looked like through winter.

Mom had failed at balancing a career and family. But both were attainable, weren't they? I could be a mother and have a career, succeeding at both, right?

Right. I closed my eyes, drawing in a few long, deep breaths.

A hand touched my shoulder and I jumped, nearly falling off the couch. I would have crashed into the floor if not for Tobias standing above me, catching me before I rolled.

"Oh my God. You scared me." I slapped a hand to my racing heart. "I thought you left."

"I did." He glanced at the wall clock. "Three hours ago."

"What?" I shoved up and looked around the room for a clock. Sure enough, the wall clock confirmed his story. Three hours had evaporated while I'd been sleeping on the couch. "Damn. I didn't even realize I'd fallen asleep. I guess I won't be working this morning."

Or this afternoon. My stomach twisted and I curled onto my side. There wasn't much to do, but I'd send my boss an email when I didn't feel like hurling.

"You okay?" Tobias asked.

"I think I jinxed myself saying I didn't get morning sickness."

A frown marred his handsome face as he stood and walked out of the living room, coming back moments later with a glass of water. He set it on the coffee table and moved to the end of the couch. "Lift up."

I raised my legs just enough for him to sit, then he positioned my calves on his lap and began massaging my foot. One touch and my eyes drifted closed, the nausea easing. Tobias's touch was magic.

"I forgot how good you are at that." I hummed.

His long fingers dug into my arch, pressing away the tension in my body. "Drink that water."

I stretched to lift it from the coaster, then sipped it slowly before setting it aside and closing my eyes again, relaxing into his touch. "How was work?"

"Fine. Quiet. I was the only one there."

"What are you working on?"

"I'm designing a house for a couple from St. Louis. They're moving to Bozeman in a year. Pretty standard floor plan except they want a bunker."

I cracked an eye. "A bunker? For what?"

"Doomsday preppers, I think. They didn't explain much, just asked for a twenty-by-twenty bunker."

"Ah." I snuggled deeper into the couch, letting his deep baritone wrap around me like a blanket. "What would you put in a twenty-by-twenty bunker?"

"Food. Water. My hunting rifle. Tools. Toilet paper."

"Tobias Practical Holiday."

He chuckled. "And what would you want in your twenty-by-twenty bunker?"

"Wine. Chocolate. Books." *You.*

If the world was ending, I'd want to be with Tobias. I'd want his arms around me through the scary nights. I'd want his strength to lean on when I felt like collapsing. I'd want his smile to brighten the dark days.

"My mom is coming to town," I said. "She called after you left."

"When?"

"Tomorrow. We're having dinner at Elena's. I get to be the buffer."

"Want me to tag along? Be your buffer?"

"No, that's okay." As tempting as it was, it would only lead to questions, mostly from Elena.

Mom had only met him once. While I'd been in college, her visits to Montana had been infrequent, at best. After the divorce, Mom and Dad hadn't needed to pretend anymore. And I think Mom knew we'd picked Dad's side so she'd stayed away, giving us all space.

But if I showed at dinner with Tobias, Elena would get her hopes up. She'd been on his wavelength, assuming we'd get married after college.

I hadn't told her that he'd proposed. I hadn't told anyone. Did he think about that night? Did he regret proposing? Did he feel like he'd dodged a bullet?

My stomach churned again. Thinking about the ring he'd bought me, the diamond on someone else's finger now, always made me queasy. "Tell me more about your projects. Keep my mind off my tummy."

"Today I was doing some drafting for Maddox's place. He's building a big place out of town. It'll be fun to spend his money."

I laughed. "What are you thinking?"

Tobias shifted, taking my other foot in his hand, and as his fingers moved over my skin, he told me about his ideas for his brother's house. From the layout to the design elements to the state-of-the-art features that would make the home a masterpiece. A theater. A pool. A guesthouse. Everything would be custom.

Excitement radiated off Tobias as he spoke. His energy was contagious, and I turned to see his face. Here was a man who genuinely loved his job. He loved his family.

"It all sounds amazing." Maybe I'd even get the chance to see it.

"I, um . . . when Maddox came into the office yesterday, I told him. About the baby."

"Oh." I wrapped my arms around my stomach. It was only a matter of time. People would need to know. I guess I hadn't planned on telling anyone until I had a better idea of what was happening.

"I can ask him to keep it quiet."

"It's okay." I lifted a shoulder. "It's not going to be a secret for long."

"Will you tell your parents or Elena?"

Dad would be thrilled. Elena would immediately start planning a baby shower. And they'd both expect me to stay.

"Probably not this trip. I'll call and tell them once I get settled in London."

Tobias's hands stopped moving. He stared at me with that same unreadable expression from this morning.

"What?" I whispered.

"Nothing." He slid out from beneath my legs and nodded to the water. "I'll be in the office down the hallway if you need anything."

I blinked and he was gone, leaving me alone. A chill settled in my bones, left by the man striding down the hallway. What was I supposed to say? I had to move. My job started next week. I had responsibilities and I'd made commitments.

He might have been comfortable sharing right away, but I was still trying to wrap my head around impending motherhood.

I pushed up and stood, ready to retreat to my bedroom and crack open my laptop. But the moment I was on my feet, another wave of nausea hit, and instead of walking, I ran to my bathroom, making it just in time to puke up the remnants of my breakfast and water. I'd thought after round one there hadn't been anything left.

Was this morning sickness? Or anxiety? It wouldn't be the first time I'd worked myself into an emotional mess. My first weeks in New York had been spent in a constant state of ick.

Headaches. Insomnia. Dizziness. Every day had been a struggle. Every day I'd wanted to quit. It was sheer stubbornness I'd gutted it out. I'd missed Tobias and home so much it had been crippling, but I'd kept pushing. Kept going. One day at a time until the heartache had eased. Until the tears had stopped.

I'd survived New York. I'd get through this too.

"Hey." Tobias appeared in the doorway, my water glass in his hand.

"Hi," I muttered.

He set my glass aside, then pulled a washcloth from a drawer, soaking it in warm water in the sink.

"Thanks." I took it from him, expecting him to leave me to my misery. But he walked closer, taking up a seat behind me. Then those wondrous hands began rubbing circles along my spine.

Sooner than later, I'd have to learn to deal with this and all the other pregnancy woes alone. But I loved his touch too much to kick him out. So I hugged the toilet, dry-heaving twice while Tobias held my hair, until finally, my stomach was empty and stopped swirling.

"I'll give you a minute." Tobias stood, easing the door shut behind him.

I washed my face and brushed my teeth, and when I emerged into the kitchen, Tobias had pulled out a box of saltine crackers. "These are for me?"

"I'll run into town and get some ginger ale. Anything else sound good?"

"Apple sauce."

"'Kay. Be back."

"Tobias?" I called as he walked toward the hall.

He stopped and turned. "Yeah?"

"You're going to be a good dad."

He gave me a sad smile, then he disappeared into the garage. His silence rang in the house. I'd expected a *thank you*. Or an *I hope so*. Maybe what I'd really wanted was for him to tell me I'd be a good mom.

But I'd learned a long time ago, Tobias didn't always tell me what I'd wanted to hear.

I guess that hadn't changed.

CHAPTER SIX

TOBIAS

E va was naked in the shower. She'd come home from dinner at her sister's place minutes ago, complaining that the smell of bacon cheeseburgers was stuck in her hair. So she'd retreated to her bathroom for a shower while I sat rigid on the couch, staring unfocused at the TV, because my attention was rapt on the woman occupying the other end of my house.

I glanced at the clock. *Eight seventeen.* In the two days since she'd come to stay here, I'd been watching the minutes pass too quickly.

She was leaving in four days and we had yet to talk about the baby. Or the kiss. The topics might not have earned a voice but lingered in the air, weighing heavy on our shoulders.

I hadn't wanted to bring it up yesterday when she'd been hugging the toilet and retching her damn guts out.

Eva hadn't gotten sick today, but before I could broach the baby topic, she'd left for work and to visit her dad over lunch.

We needed to talk. Except I wasn't sure what to say.

Stay? Don't move? I hadn't asked her to stay after the proposal from hell. There hadn't been a point. Her mind had been made up then, as I suspected it was now.

No, our conversation needed to be about custody. Every time that word rang in my head, I cringed. I was going to push for the baby to live here. To be in Montana full-time, surrounded not just by my family, but hers too.

That was the only option. She had to know that was the only option.

"What a clusterfuck," I muttered.

"What?"

I spun around, seeing Eva halfway between the hallway and living room. Her hair was wet and twisted in a knot. Her slender body was covered in a set of baggy gray sweats.

"Nothing." I nodded to the TV where ESPN was playing football highlights. "My team lost," I lied.

"Oh." She sighed and came around the couch, curling up in the same end where she'd napped yesterday.

"How was dinner?"

"Okay." She shrugged. "Elena focused on her girls and cooking. Her husband and I answered Mom's questions. You know how she is. And I guess she moved."

"She did? Where?"

"Salt Lake. Good thing I didn't send a Christmas present to her old place in Florida."

I shook my head. Eddy Williams was a damn good man. Elena was sweet and kind. But I could do without Michelle.

Eva had patience for her mother, more than Michelle deserved. In four years of college, she'd come to see Eva once. We'd gone out to dinner and Michelle had asked so many questions I'd felt like it had been an interrogation. It was like she'd wanted to cram years of missed conversations into a single meal. One dinner, then she'd flown away, off to her life in the sky, and then occasionally sent Eva a text to check in.

From the sounds of it, nothing had changed. Michelle lived her life. Everyone else was ancillary.

"Elena and I decided not to tell Dad she was in town. It bothers him."

"Do they talk?"

"I don't think so. She called him after his stroke, but otherwise . . . not that I know of."

"Do you talk often? You and your dad?"

She nodded. "Almost every day. I usually text Elena a few times a week and FaceTime with her and the girls on Sundays."

Is that why she didn't think living across the country with my baby was going to be a problem? Because she'd made it work with her dad and sister?

This was not the same situation. Eddy might be okay

with it because Eva was a grown woman, but I refused to have a relationship with my child via FaceTime. It was on the tip of my tongue to tell her exactly that, but instead, I reached for the remote and changed the channel.

Yeah, we needed to talk.

But I didn't want to.

There was no way this discussion ended happily.

"Feel like a movie?" I asked.

"Sure." She curled her legs into the seat, sinking into a toss pillow. "I might get a snack. I wasn't really hungry at dinner."

"What do you feel like? Chips? Cookies? Carrot sticks?"

"Hey, watch your language."

I blinked. "What did I say?"

"Carrot sticks." Her face soured. "How about popcorn?"

"Popcorn it is. You pick the movie." I tossed her the remote and retreated to the kitchen, needing some distance. That sweet, soft scent was too enticing.

With a bowl of popcorn for us to share, I put it between us and handed her a throw blanket. "Here."

"How'd you know I was cold?"

Because I knew her. Or I had once. "Are you?"

"Yes." She swiped it from my hand, draping it over her legs. Then she grabbed a handful of popcorn and turned up the volume on the TV. "We're watching a Hallmark movie. This one just started."

"Seriously?"

"It's December, Tobias. They only play these once a year."

Which meant she'd watch Hallmark or nothing.

"Fine." We'd have enough to argue about shortly. Tonight, I wasn't going to bicker over *A Cowboy Christmas*.

Eva inhaled the popcorn, eating most of the bowl before she'd realized I hadn't had a kernel. "Do you not want any?"

"Nah. I did my workout already." I'd come home earlier to an empty house that smelled like Eva. I'd needed to burn some energy, so I'd turned around, climbed back in my truck, and headed to the gym.

"Afraid you'll lose the six-pack?" Her gaze dragged down my body, her eyes darkening.

Eva loved my six-pack. She loved the definition at my hips and the strength of my arms. And that look on her face . . . fuck. That was the look that usually landed us in bed.

I scooped a handful of popcorn and shoved it in my mouth, willing myself with every crunch to stay on this side of the couch. Except I wasn't hungry for anything but her.

She squirmed, inching closer to her own armrest. We both faced the TV just in time to see the couple on screen kiss.

Fuck my life.

I hadn't been this sexually frustrated since I'd been sixteen at a friend's house party where all of the senior-year cheerleaders had decided to skinny-dip in the hot tub.

But there was nothing to do but suffer. The movie dragged on and on, and about an hour in, Eva set the empty popcorn bowl aside, then shifted, moving closer to the middle of the couch.

She yawned three times and with each, inched my way. On the fourth, she let out a groan.

"What's wrong?"

"I can't get comfortable."

I threw an arm over the back of the couch. "Come on over."

She didn't hesitate. The space between us vanished and she curled into my side. It took all of sixty seconds until she was asleep.

The remote was too far away for me to reach without waking her up, so I sat and watched the rest of the Hallmark movie, enduring this fictional couple's journey to a happily ever after while Eva's wet hair soaked my shirt.

When the movie was over, I leaned deeper into the couch and stared at the ceiling. What if this was our life? Was it really so bad? Couldn't she be happy here?

No. She'd had her chance at this and had walked away. I wouldn't make the mistake of getting on one knee again only to be kicked in the face.

I blew out a deep breath and shifted, tucking my arms beneath her knees and shoulders. Then in one swoop, I stood from the couch, Eva in my arms, and carried her to the guest bedroom.

"Is the movie over?" she murmured, her eyes still closed.

"Finally."

"Was it good?"

"No."

"Liar," she whispered. "You love Christmas movies."

I chuckled and stepped into the dark room, taking her to the bed. "Sleep tight."

With a quick kiss to her forehead, I moved to step away, but her hand snagged mine.

"Tobias?" Her eyes opened and those hazel pools were my undoing.

She didn't say another word. She didn't have to. We'd done this dance a hundred times.

I swept her into my arms, shifting us both deeper into the bed.

The moment my lips hit hers I fell into the deep end and drowned.

Eva let out a small mewl as my tongue tangled with hers, her sweetness mixed with a hint of salt from the popcorn. I licked and sucked and nipped until she was clawing at my back, tugging at my shirt.

I settled into the cradle of her hips, pressing my arousal into her core and swallowing her gasp before tearing my lips away. "Babe, tell me to stop."

"Don't stop." Her hands trailed lower, her palms

molding to the curve of my ass before she gave it a hard squeeze.

I arched into her, earning a moan, then trailed my lips down the long column of her throat. My hands slipped beneath the hem of her sweatshirt and skimmed up her ribs. My knuckles grazed the swell of her breasts. "Eva."

"Tobias."

My name in her voice, laced with heat, and my cock throbbed. "Last warning."

She answered by letting go of my ass to cup my erection through my zipper. "Don't. Stop."

I lifted off of her, working my shirt free. Then I yanked the sweatshirt from her body, sending it sailing to the floor. Her pants and panties came next until every inch of her smooth skin was on display.

Eva lifted and frantically loosened the buttons on my jeans. She freed me from my boxers, wrapping her hand around my shaft.

"Christ." I savored the feel of her hand for a few strokes before I moved away, standing to strip.

Eva watched my every move, her eyes flaring with lust as they dragged down my stomach. That look right there was worth every minute in the gym and each mile on the treadmill.

I planted a knee on the bed and settled between her thighs before trailing a hand over her thigh and down her calf, taking it in my hand and hooking her leg around my waist. "What do you want?"

"You."

I was one second away from thrusting deep and hard when my gaze landed on her belly. My baby was in there. Ours. In months we'd have a baby.

"What?" Eva propped up on an elbow.

"This. Us." I nodded to her stomach. "You good with this?"

Eva dropped her leg and shoved up to a seat. Then with a fast shove, pushed me over and onto my back until she straddled my hips. One hand stayed planted on my sternum while she positioned me at her entrance with the other, sinking down until I was sheathed.

"Fuck." I thrust my hips up, burying myself in her tight heat.

"Oh, God." She squeezed her eyes closed as her inner walls fluttered.

Every fucking time it was amazing. Like her body had been made to fit mine.

"Move," I ordered, taking her hips and lifting her so she could slam back down.

The worries, the fears, were all shoved aside as she rode me, over and over until her legs began to tremble.

With a twist, I reversed our positions, putting her back to the mattress so I could work in and out of her pussy, stroke after stroke until she writhed beneath me.

Her hands fisted the bedding. Her teeth held her bottom lip. Her limbs tensed.

"Let go, Eva."

She shook her head. "Not yet."

"Goddamn it, come."

"Together," she breathed.

I growled and thrust faster until the pressure was too much to resist. "Come."

One touch of my thumb to her clit and she detonated. She pulsed around me, her orgasm triggering my own, and I poured into her, long and hard until we were both boneless.

I collapsed on the bed beside her. "Damn."

"Wow." Her chest heaved as she regained her breath.

The stars in my eyes took minutes to clear, and after my heart stopped racing, I jackknifed off the bed and went to the bathroom, getting a cloth to clean her up.

Instead, her footsteps followed. "Take a shower with me."

"We could go to mine. It's twice this size."

She shook her head and turned on the water. It took only seconds to warm since she'd been in here not that long ago, and when she took my hand, I followed her willingly beneath the water.

Her hands slid up and down my body as steam surrounded us. She lifted to her toes, wanting my mouth.

She didn't get it. Instead, I spun her around, gripped her hips and slid inside once more, losing myself in the woman who had me twisted in a knot.

We fucked slow and deep until we both came on a cry.

Then I squeezed some soap on the shower puff and scrubbed our bodies clean.

The mirror was fogged when we toweled off. I kept one tied around my waist as Eva retreated to the bedroom to pull on her clothes.

She climbed into bed, patting the space beside her. "Will you cuddle with me, baby?"

It had been a long damn time since she'd called me baby. Not even during our night six weeks ago had she let that old endearment slip. And that single word sent a jolt of ice through my veins.

"What are we doing?" I whispered.

"Huh?" She yawned.

"Eva, what are we doing? You're calling me *baby*. We're fucking. Cuddling. What are we doing?"

Her shoulders fell. Her gaze dropped to the blankets over her lap. "I don't know. We're in a pickle, aren't we?"

"Pretty much." I huffed. "We have to figure this out."

"Would you move?"

"To where? London?"

She shrugged. "It would be an adventure."

"I don't need an adventure." This baby would be undertaking enough. I opened my mouth to ask her to stay but clamped it shut before the words escaped.

I wouldn't ask. Not when I knew the answer.

Eva stared at me, waiting. Like she could see my restraint. Like the unspoken question floated through the air like the scent of the shower. When she realized I wasn't going to say anything, she dropped her gaze again. "So then I guess it's FaceTime and Santa's sleigh."

My throat felt tight as I moved to sweep up my clothes and stalk out of the room.

FaceTime. Airports. Long-distance. Those were her solutions. What the hell had I been thinking tonight? Sex was complicated and intimate and . . . it made sense.

Why couldn't she see how much sense we made? How good our life could be? How good we were together?

I was a fucking fool. She'd leave me again. Just like she had before.

This time, with my child.

CHAPTER SEVEN

EVA

"I'm sending you my final report as we speak." My fingers flew over my laptop's keyboard as I talked to my boss with my phone sandwiched between my ear and shoulder. "I stopped by the site this morning and everything looks polished. The cleaning crew did a great job. The clients are happy. We should be good to close this project out."

"Thanks, Eva," he said. "You did a fantastic job coming to the rescue, as always. All set for next week?"

"Yes." My insides churned at the lie.

Six days ago, yes. Absolutely, yes. I'd been ready for London. Then that pregnancy test had changed everything and I wasn't sure what to be excited about.

"Fantastic." His keyboard clicked in the background. "Just got your email. I'll reply if I have any questions. Touch base when you get to London."

"Will do. Thanks." I ended the call and set my phone on the island, staring at my empty inbox.

Normally zero emails would mean a happy dance and takeout dinner to celebrate. So why did I want to curl up in a ball and cry?

This was Tobias's fault. He'd given me two orgasms last night and now I was an emotional mess. Or maybe it was the baby's fault, which was actually his fault because his sperm had escaped the confines of a condom.

"Stupid sperm," I muttered, shooting a glare down the hallway toward his bedroom.

When I'd woken up this morning, the house had been silent. I'd tiptoed toward his office, peeking my head through the door. When I'd found it empty, I'd snuck toward his bedroom, finding it empty as well. Then I'd double-checked the garage and my car had been alone in the last stall.

He hadn't even left a note.

"Isn't the mother of his child and the woman he just had sex with entitled to a note? I bet he left notes for his other girlfriends."

My stomach roiled again. *Don't think about his other girlfriends. Do not think about his other girlfriends.*

Eventually he'd start dating, right? I was going to have to deal with that at some point. Eventually my baby would have to meet the next woman. A stepmother.

"Oh, shit." The bowl of bran flakes I'd scarfed for breakfast began its climb. I barely made it to the bathroom in time to hurl, then lingered on the cool tile floor until I felt steady again. My gaze drifted to the shower.

Okay, so maybe sex with Tobias had been a tad . . . reckless. But the minute he'd kissed me, rational thought had vanished, replaced by an urgent craving for more, more, *more.*

"Damn him and those washboard abs." I shoved to my feet and went to the sink to brush my teeth. Again. Then I retreated to the kitchen to shut down my laptop and sign off for the day. Maybe I'd visit Dad or Elena.

I was filling a glass of water when the doorbell rang. A familiar face peered in through the sidelight.

Hannah Holiday didn't seem at all surprised to see me staring back.

I crossed the space and unlocked the door, smiling as I pulled it open. "Hey, Hannah."

"Eva!" She set her purse on the floor and pulled me into her arms. "Oh, it's so good to see you."

"You too."

She smelled like gardenia and brown sugar, the scent as strong and comforting as her hug.

"I've missed your hugs," she said, finally letting me go.

"I've missed yours too."

Hannah had been like a mother to me during college. My junior year, I'd gotten a nasty cold, and the day Tobias told her I was sick, she'd showed up at my apartment door and had whisked me away to her home where she'd nursed me back to health with homemade chicken noodle soup.

She'd been there for me when my own mother hadn't.

And then I'd lost her too.

That was something no one warned you about when you started dating. That you'd begin to love your boyfriend's family. And that when you lost him, you lost his family too.

"I've brought you something." She held up a finger, then bent to rifle through her purse, coming out with a bag of ginger lollipops. "In case you get sick."

"Thanks." My nose was stinging, but I sniffled it away before I cried. "Tobias told you?"

"No, not exactly. He told Maddox, who let it slip at breakfast this morning. Sorry."

"It's okay." It was bound to come out sometime, but that meant I needed to tell my family before long. The last thing I wanted was for Dad or Elena to hear it through the gossip mill.

Bozeman had changed a lot over the years since I'd moved away, but at its heart, this was still a small town. And the Holidays were one of the most successful families in the valley.

Hannah was a real estate broker, her face on dozens of for-sale signs. Her brokerage was well-known and well-respected because they sold the best properties, including those built from Holiday Homes.

Keith had started his construction company decades ago and had grown it to be one of the most premier companies in the area. With Tobias designing their builds, I had no doubt that Keith's legacy would live long.

"So tell me what's new." Hannah walked into the house, stripping off her coat and tossing it to the back of the couch before she moved to the kitchen, finding the single-brew pods and making herself some coffee.

"Well . . . I'm pregnant." I laughed. "It's strange. I haven't said those words out loud to anyone but Tobias."

"Give it time. Soon you won't have to say a thing." She smiled, opening the fridge to retrieve some cream. With her nearly white coffee, she came and sat at my side. "How are you feeling?"

"Some days are better than others. My morning sickness seems sporadic." If it was even morning sickness. The days when my heart and head were in the most turmoil, seemed to translate to my stomach.

"It'll pass. I didn't have those lollipops when I was pregnant with the boys, but one of my agents just had her third and she swears by them."

"Thank you."

"Hopefully you can find them in London. If not, text me and I'll stick some in the mail."

"Okay." Just the mention of London made my insides twist again.

Was I doing this? Was I really leaving home again? If there was a person in the world to talk about my doubts with, it was Hannah. When I looked at her, she was the mother I wanted to be someday.

She had a flourishing career. She was a fantastic parent. She had found that magical balance. How?

I opened my mouth, ready to ask, but stopped myself. Hannah was Tobias's. She was his mother, not mine. If I dragged her into this mess, it would only put her in a tough position. I didn't want her to be the mediator if he went to her with his own frustrations and fears. I didn't want her feeling responsible to play both sides.

So I stuck to a safe topic. Work. "How is business?"

"Busy." She blew out a long breath. "So busy. But a good kind of busy. Any chance you want to become an agent? I could use a smart cookie like you."

"Oh, um . . ." I scrunched up my nose. Selling homes sounded more like torture. "No, thanks."

"Damn." She winked. "I was secretly hoping that you have been dying for a career in real estate."

"If that changes, you'll be my first phone call." I giggled.

"Oh, it's so good to hear your laugh. Tell me more about what you've been doing. Are you excited for London? How is your dad?"

We spent the next hour catching up. Not once did Hannah ask me about the baby. Not once did she comment about how nice it would be if her grandchild lived in the same country. Not once did she ask how Tobias and I were going to handle the situation.

She simply talked to me the way she'd talked to me years ago. Like a daughter.

Like a friend.

The hum of the garage door halted our conversation.

Tobias walked in and found us both at the island. He went straight to his mom, not sparing me a glance, and kissed her cheek. "Hey."

"Hi." She patted his beard. "Where were you?"

"The office. What's up?"

"Nothing." She stood from her stool and carried her empty coffee mug to the dishwasher. "I just wanted to say hi."

"Hi." He leaned against the counter, his back to me. There was stiffness to his spine, likely caused by me.

"I'll leave you guys alone to visit." I slid off my seat. "It was so good to see you, Hannah."

"You too, honey." She came over and gave me another hug. "And congratulations."

"Thanks." I squeezed my eyes shut so I wouldn't cry.

She was the first to say congratulations. And it struck me right then, with her arms around me, that there was more here to be excited about than to fear.

I was having a baby.

Oh, God. I was having a baby.

Maybe he or she would have my hazel eyes. Maybe Tobias's straight nose and soft lips. The idea of a miniature Tobias Holiday put a small smile on my face.

"Love you," she whispered.

"Love you too."

"See you soon," Hannah said, letting me go.

"Okay." I waved and left the kitchen, feeling Tobias's gaze as I retreated to the guest bedroom where I hovered inside the door, hearing him blow out a long breath.

"So I take it Maddox told you," he said.

"Yeah." Hannah sighed. "You doing okay?"

"No."

That one word, barely audible, hit like a sledge-hammer to my sternum.

I eased the door closed behind me, not because I wasn't curious about their conversation, but because I wasn't sure I had the strength to hear Tobias's truths.

"Oof." I plopped onto the edge of the bed and pinched the bridge of my nose.

My phone and laptop were still in the kitchen, so all I could do was sit and wait, letting the minutes pass until finally the front door closed, and from beyond the windows, a car engine started.

It wouldn't always be like this. It would get easier as we had more time to adjust. All major life decisions took time to comprehend. Maybe coming up with a plan—Tobias would do cartwheels when I tossed out that word—would help ease the stress.

I could book an airline ticket to fly back in two months. Or three? Would I have time for a trip home by then? Would Tobias want to come to London? When would we be able to find out the sex of the baby? How often would I go to the doctor?

As the questions raced through my mind, I realized

how woefully unprepared I was for a pregnancy. My stomach began another round of dizzying laps, and I shoved to my feet, hoping one of Hannah's lollipops might help. But after one step, I gagged and changed directions for the bathroom.

There wasn't anything in my stomach but I dry-heaved and coughed regardless.

"Oh, this sucks." I groaned. Sweat beaded on my forehead as I shifted to lean against the wall. My entire body felt twisted inside out. My muscles were somehow locked but trembling. My head was spinning and I wanted to cry.

So I did.

I buried my face in my hands and cried. I let the emotions leak down my face. I let the fears sob from my mouth.

There was no reason I should feel so lonely here. I was at home. My dad was ten minutes away. So was Elena. But this bathroom felt like a black hole. Just me and my baby. Just me and the soul-deep fear that I was going to fail. I was going to let this kid down.

How was I going to do this? How was I going to be a good mom? Tobias didn't believe in me. Hell, I didn't believe in myself.

I was crying so hard that I didn't hear the door open.

One moment I was on the cool tile, the next I was against Tobias's chest as he swept me into his arms. "Breathe, babe."

I nodded, too far gone to stop. But instead of crying

into my hands alone, I cried into his shoulder as he carried me to the bed and cradled me in his lap. "I hate this."

"It'll get better. Morning sickness doesn't last forever."

"It's not that. At least, I don't think." I pulled away, wiping my face dry and sniffling through the last of the tears.

Except this queasy feeling originated from my heart. The magnitude of what we were facing was breaking me into pieces.

Stress didn't bother me. Hell, I thrived on it. I'd made a career of thriving on it. But the anxiety . . . God, the anxiety was paralyzing.

"I don't know." I moved out of his lap and into the space between his spread legs, hugging my knees to my chest.

He tucked a lock of my hair behind an ear. "When we were younger, I think we took for granted how well we knew each other."

"What do you mean?"

"I mean, we didn't have to talk. You could look at me and, most days, know exactly what I was thinking or how I was feeling. It was always . . . easy."

"I loved that about us." I gave him a small smile. Tobias was the one person who always made it easy.

"Yeah, me too. But it meant we didn't fight."

"You want to fight? Okay, I think the paint color you picked for this room is too gray. It's boring."

He chuckled. "You really want to fight about paint colors?"

"You just asked me to fight with you."

"Woman." He shook his head, a grin on his lips. "My point . . . I think we got used to it being so good. I think we were happy. And then we didn't do anything to fuck it up. Like talk to each other. Or let it get messy."

I sighed. "I should have told you I wanted to move."

"Yeah, you should have." There was a sharpness to his voice, a tone that slashed straight to the bone. Every cell in my body went on edge.

This was exactly the feeling I'd get during the rare times we had argued. It made me want to hurl all over again. *Wow.* How had I not realized that before? He was right. So damn right.

I hated it when Tobias was angry with me. *Hated. It.* So I'd done everything in my power to avoid a fight, including hiding my dreams.

Hiding had only lasted so long. And in the end, the truth had finally come to light.

"Don't hate me," I whispered, my eyes locking with his. "I won't survive it."

"I could never hate you." He caught a new tear with his thumb and brushed it away. "But I can be pissed at you. You can be pissed at me. And we can get to the other side by talking it out. So talk to me. Tell me what's going on in your head."

I sagged, the air rushing from my lungs. "I don't want to give up my job."

Oof. That confession felt like walking down Main Street buck-ass naked.

It shouldn't have been so hard to say. Tobias was just as committed to his career as I was to mine. But I guess, deep down, I was still the woman who'd felt it necessary to hide her dreams. The one woman who'd chosen that job over him. The one who feared he'd never truly forgive me for breaking us apart.

"It's my identity," I told him. "I'm not sure who I am without it anymore. It saved me when I was at my lowest. And it's more than the money, it's my pride."

"Hey." Tobias hooked his finger under my chin, lifting it so I could meet his gaze. Then there it was, the familiar comfort in his eyes. The understanding that he knew what it was like to love a job. To have a career fill a void.

A void that I'd created in his life when I'd left Montana.

The energy seemed to leave my body at once, like a light being turned off with a flick of a switch. I barely had the strength to scoot to the pillows and collapse.

Tobias stretched out beside me, his body on one half of the bed, mine on the other. There was a clear line between us, his pillows, my pillows. Except for one touch. He took my hand, lacing our fingers together, and held it tight until I drifted off to sleep.

A ding woke me up, my head fuzzy as I lifted off the

pillow. I shoved the hair out of my face and swung my legs off the bed, taking a few long breaths before getting to my feet.

I braced for a wave of nausea that never came. My stomach felt solid as a rock. Normal. Maybe what I'd needed wasn't lollipops and saltines, but a release. To talk it out with Tobias.

To fight, if that got us to a better place.

I shuffled out of the room and down the hallway, my bare feet quiet on the hardwood floors. The flip of the door's lock gave an audible pop. Then came a woman's voice.

"Hey. I know I should have called first but I thought . . . what the hell? I'd take the chance you were home and had a few hours free."

"Chelsea . . ."

Chelsea? Wait. One of my friends from college was named Chelsea, but I hadn't spoken to her in years.

"I know, you hate surprises. I'll make it up to you in bed."

What. The. Fuck.

Tobias did hate surprises. I wasn't a fan of them myself.

Especially when the surprise was a pretty blonde standing in the entryway with her lips on Tobias's mouth.

CHAPTER EIGHT

TOBIAS

"Chelsea." I pushed her away before she could do more than brush her lips to mine.

"Oh, dang." She deflated. "Bad time?"

"Yeah." I gave her a sad smile. "I think . . . we'd better call it quits. Sorry."

"It's fine. I'll get out of your hair." She waved it off, her car keys rattling in her hand as she spun for the door.

But before she could step out into the bright afternoon sun, I caught her elbow. "Happy New Year."

"Happy New Year, Tobias. Call me if you ever want to start this up again."

I nodded, stood in the cold and waited until her car reversed out of the driveway. "Shit."

Of all the weeks for Chelsea to arrive, this was the one she'd picked. But even if she'd come next week or the next or the next, I would have sent her away.

With Eva . . . everything was different now. There was no going back to cheap hookups and casual flings. Chelsea was a nice woman with a pretty smile and kind heart. She'd kept me company.

But she wasn't Eva.

No one was.

I closed the door, ready to retreat to my office for a few hours of work in the hopes of getting my mind off the shit swirling in my personal life, but as I turned, a pair of angry hazel eyes halted my escape.

"Chelsea?" Eva tapped her foot in rapid succession. *Pat. Pat. Pat.* Yep, she was furious. "Really?"

Fuck. "It's nothing."

She arched an eyebrow.

"It was casual. Just an occasional . . ." *Hookup.* I stopped myself, fear for my testicles if I finished that sentence. "She lives in Billings. Every few months she comes here for work and we go to dinner."

"Like the dinner we went on." She scoffed, then spun and stormed down the hallway.

"Damn it." I hurried to follow, finding her sitting on her bed, legs crossed, arms folded and a death glare on her face. She was the epitome of livid, quivering chin and all. "Eva. It's nothing. It's been months. Before you and I had dinner."

"Don't." She closed her eyes. "I don't want to know."

"Okay." I held up a hand, ready to leave, but her eyes snapped open and that murderous glare found me again.

"Chelsea? How many other friends of mine have there been?"

Here we go. "Just Chelsea."

"I—grr." She huffed. "I can't even be mad."

"Then why are you?"

"Because." She tossed out a hand and leapt off the bed, marching to the bathroom. Drawers were ripped open and slammed, one after another. When I braved the threshold, I found her brushing her hair in a rage.

"Talk to me." Was I always going to have to beg for her to tell me how she felt?

She kept on brushing. "Because it's not fair."

"What's not fair?"

"That you've moved on." The brush went sailing to the counter, clattering as it slid and dropped into the empty sink. "It's not fair. I don't want you to move on. The idea of you with another woman, with a Chelsea or Tiffany or, or, or whoever, makes my skin crawl."

"What do you want me to say?" I raked a hand through my hair. "You left. You left me."

"I know!" Her eyes flooded. "I know I left. And you moved on. But I didn't."

"Wait." I held up a finger. "What are you saying?"

"Never mind." She blew past me through the door, and before I could make sense of what she'd just told me, she was gone.

The garage door opened and closed, followed by the crunch of her tires on the snow as she drove away.

She hadn't moved on. Seriously? So she hadn't been with anyone else? But it had been years. What the fuck did that mean?

"Son of a bitch." I unglued my feet and followed the path she took. Out the door, into my truck and away. Just away.

I'd asked Eva to fight with me. *Stupid fucking idea, Holiday.* I sure as shit didn't feel like doing it again.

So I drove around town for hours until the sun had long set and my tires led me to my brother's house. Heath had been calling me for days. I'd avoided him, mostly because I still wasn't sure what to say.

Or maybe because I suspected what Heath *would* say.

He'd tell me to go with her.

Before I could knock or ring the bell, Heath opened the door. "Hey. What's going on? I've been calling you."

"Yeah." I stomped my feet and walked into the house, straight to the kitchen. It smelled like dinner and my stomach growled. An open bottle of cabernet rested on the counter.

Heath stood behind me, arms crossed and his forehead furrowed. Apparently, Maddox and Mom hadn't told him what was happening with Eva.

Probably a good thing. Maybe if I said it out loud again, I'd find a way to make sense of it all.

So I nodded to the bottle. "Got any more of that wine?"

"WHERE THE HELL IS SHE?" I muttered, glancing out the living room window for the hundredth time.

I hadn't seen Eva all day.

Last night, I'd lingered at Heath's place, mostly because I didn't trust myself after dark with Eva under the same roof. Either we'd pick up the argument, sit in awkward silence or fuck.

Every moment with her was laced with an undercurrent of desire. I craved her more and more, and the other night had barely taken the edge off. If she gave me the slightest opening, I'd take it.

So I'd sat on my brother's couch, mindlessly watching a game on TV, and thought about everything he'd had to say.

Talk to her. Go with her.

We're your family no matter where you live.

There's no reason you have to live here to help run the company.

Every time I'd voice a concern, whether it be distance from family or working remotely for Holiday Homes, he'd countered with advice I hadn't wanted to hear.

Could I move? Could I live in London for a year? Then bounce to wherever it was she went next? What the hell kind of life was that?

"Not for me." My hands fisted as I paced the length of

the living room. My eyes once more drifted to the windows and black sky beyond.

Her suitcase was still in the guest bedroom so at least she hadn't moved out. She had to come back sometime, right?

It was ten. Twenty more minutes and I was calling. This close to New Year's with ice on the roads, I didn't want her out alone on a Friday night. Would she keep these kinds of hours in London? She needed sleep. Our baby needed her to be well rested.

The seconds ticked by so slowly I was about to lose my shit, until finally the flash of headlights bounced through the glass and the garage door rattled open.

I was at the door before she could get out of the driver's seat of her sedan. "Hi."

"Hi." She walked toward me with her eyes on the floor.

"Are you okay? I was getting worried."

"Fine." Her eyes stayed on my shoulder, not my face, as she slipped past me into the house. "Tired. I'm going to go to bed. Night."

No. We weren't going another night without talking. "Eva."

"Please, Tobias." Her shoulders slumped as she turned. "I can't argue with you."

"I don't want to argue."

"Then what? What do you want?"

You. To stay. The words I couldn't bring myself to say.

"I don't want to miss this. I want to be able to tell our kid stories about when you were pregnant. I want to be the nervous dad at the doctor's appointments. I want the ultrasound photo to carry in my wallet. I'd like to figure out a way to make that happen."

"I'm open to ideas."

"I went to Heath's last night. He suggested hitting up Maddox for a jet since he can afford it."

A ghost of a smile crossed her pretty lips. "What else did Heath say?"

"That we both want the best for our kid. So we'll figure it out."

"We will. Maybe not tonight, but we will."

For a man who loved long-term plans and five-year goals, the unknown was unnerving. But the dark circles under her eyes made my chest squeeze. "We've got tomorrow, right?"

She nodded. "I'm going to see Dad. Say goodbye. I'll probably swing by Elena's too."

"Then tomorrow night. You and me. We'll ring in the new year. I'll get some sparkling grape juice, and we'll make a real party of it."

Her eyes dropped to my lips for a split second before she tore them away, looking to her tennis shoes. "Okay. Good night."

God, I hated seeing her walk away. Even if it was just to another bedroom in my own damn house.

"Eva."

She stopped and glanced over her shoulder. "Yeah?"

"Did you find it?"

"Find what?" She turned fully, her head cocking to the side.

"Whatever it was that you were looking for in New York." Whatever dream she'd needed to chase.

"I don't know." She lifted a shoulder. "Living there was an experience. And because of my job, I've had the chance to explore a lot of places I otherwise wouldn't have found."

"Which city was your favorite?"

"Nashville."

"Because you love country music."

She smiled, moving to the island and pulling out a stool. "Any chance I got, I did all the touristy stuff with no shame. It was a blast."

"How long were you there?" I went to sit beside her. Right beside her. There was no stool to keep us apart this time because I couldn't bear the distance.

We'd have plenty of distance soon enough.

"Three months," she said. "Sort of the same assignment as I've had here. I stepped in to help with a project in trouble."

"Ah. What was your least favorite place?"

"New York," she whispered.

I sat up straighter. "What?"

"It was a hard year. I was new to the job and had a lot

of learning to do. The hours were brutal. The client was a complete jackass. And I was lonely. I missed you."

Well . . . fuck. That hit me square in the chest. "I missed you too."

"I never wanted to hurt you." She looked up, her hazel eyes full of regret. "To hurt us."

"I know."

"You do?"

I nodded. "Not gonna lie, I was pretty angry at you for a while. And I sort of nursed my anger because it was the only way I could keep a part of you."

A flash of pain crossed her face.

"Then I ran into your dad."

"You did? When?"

"About two years after you left. You were in Florida."

"Tampa. For about eight weeks. I was so busy that I didn't get to visit the beach once."

"Maybe we could go one day. The three of us." Our strange little family unit could take a vacation together.

"I'd like that," she whispered.

"Anyway. Back to your dad. I was downtown, meeting my parents for dinner. They were running late so I was sitting at the restaurant's bar and he came walking over. I guess he was on a date."

"He was?" Her mouth fell open. "I had no idea that he went on dates."

"This one was not a good date." I chuckled. "Probably

why you never heard about it. I was his excuse to get away from the table. Apparently, his date picked her nose right as their salads were delivered and the booger was put in the cloth napkin, as green as the lettuce they were about to eat."

Eva laughed. "Eww."

"He was so funny about it. He leaned in close, told me the whole story, and asked if it was rude to dump her before dessert."

"What did you say?"

"I told him to pay the check and scram."

"Did he?"

"He stayed the whole meal, even bought her a piece of chocolate cake." Eddy wasn't the kind of man who cut a date short. He treated women the way he wanted men to treat his daughters.

"That's sweet." She smiled. "I can't believe he never told me about that. Or that he saw you. What else did you talk about?"

"You. He told me you were living in Tampa but traveling all over. That you were kicking ass and taking names at your job. That he was so proud of you for taking a leap of faith."

Eddy was the first one to talk to me about Eva after the breakup. He hadn't pandered to my broken heart like my parents. He hadn't avoided bringing her name into a conversation like my brother. He'd bragged about his daughter, unabashedly.

"It was hard to stay angry at you after that. Mostly I just wanted you to be happy."

"Thank you," she breathed. "I worried for a long time that you hated me."

"Never." Angry, yes. But I'd never hated her. It just wasn't inside me.

My only hope was if I pushed for the baby to live here, she wouldn't be able to hate me either.

"That's good because you're stuck with me now." She forced a too-bright smile, lifting her chin. Then she slid off the stool. "I'd better let you get some sleep. Night."

"Wait," I blurted. "Earlier, when Chelsea was here. You said you weren't with anyone. Why?" I could probably guess, but tonight, I wanted to hear it.

"I just . . . wasn't." She shrugged. "Work was busy. And no one compared to you."

"Eva." My hand reached out and caught hers. A zing raced up my forearm at the touch. "They're always electric, aren't they?"

She nodded, her lips parting. Was that an invitation?

This was only going to get more complicated. The right thing to do would be to let her go. Leave her to her room while I locked myself in my own.

Instead, I leaned down and brushed my lips across hers, the hitch of her breath my reward.

Reward enough for one night.

It took restraint to let her go. It took every ounce of willpower to stand and take a step away.

Maybe I would have made it behind my closed door. But before I could slip my fingers free from Eva's, she tugged me back.

That string between us was as tight as ever.

This time there was no mistaking her body language as her tongue darted out and licked her bottom lip.

"Fuck it." I slammed my mouth on hers, my tongue sweeping inside. I devoured her, exploring her mouth, memorizing every corner. I held her to me, hoping that if I held tight enough, this might all make sense.

She broke away first, her eyes hooded and her lips swollen.

Fuck, but I wanted her. I wanted her for good. To keep.

But she wasn't mine.

She was her own woman. That was what Eddy had called her that night years ago. Her own woman.

So I took one step away. Then another. And this time, I made it to my bedroom without looking back.

CHAPTER NINE

EVA

"Sleep. Go. To. Sleep." I punched my pillow and flopped onto my back. The bedroom was pitch black as I yawned. But did sleep come? Nope. Not even a wink. The last time I'd checked my phone, it had been after midnight.

I should have hit the pillow and crashed. My day had been long and exhausting. Avoiding Tobias had been harder than the boot camp I'd taken a few years ago in Denver. Plus I'd slept like crap last night too, tossing and turning until Tobias had finally come home. Most of my sleepless hours had been spent wondering if he'd been with Chelsea. Freaking Chelsea. That was going to rub me like sandpaper for a long, long time.

Thank God, he'd been at his brother's.

After all that stress, I should have slept straight until

eight. Instead, I'd been lying here for hours replaying Tobias's words from earlier.

He just wanted me to be happy.

Was I happy? I hadn't asked myself that question lately. Maybe because I was scared of the answer.

I was *mostly* happy. I was happy in my job. I loved my job, almost every day. Sure, my personal life was a little dull. I moved too often to have best friends. But that was what Elena was for. Okay, so we didn't have nearly enough in common to be *best* friends. Our independent personalities often clashed, but I loved my sister.

The closest I'd ever had to a best friend was Tobias.

And he wanted me to be happy.

"Well, is he happy that I can't sleep and it's all his fault?" I jammed an elbow into the mattress and pushed myself up. "Ugh."

Maybe if he'd stop kissing me, I could get some sleep.

My mind was spinning and my body was strung as tight as a rubber band, about to snap. And damn it, this was all Tobias's fault.

He'd worked me into this turned-on, fidgeting, hormonal mess.

I whipped the covers off my legs and climbed out of bed. The cool air brought goose bumps to my arms and legs as I walked out of the bedroom and down the hall toward the couch. Maybe a Hallmark movie would lull me into dreamland.

But as I reached the kitchen, my path veered toward his bedroom. Toward the soft white glow coming from beneath his door.

I held my breath, creeping closer until I could lean my ear against the frame. The sound of rustled sheets and muted huffs brought a smile to my lips. I guess I wasn't the only one not sleeping.

We could talk. Why wait until tomorrow if we were both awake? So I rapped my knuckles on the door and turned the knob.

Tobias sat up straighter as I stepped inside. His nightstand lamp was on and a book dangled from his fingers. His chest was bare, all of that glorious muscle on display. His hair was sticking up at odd angles.

He looked . . . like my dreamland.

"You kissed me and now I can't sleep."

He tossed the book aside, his gaze tracking my every step as I rounded the foot of his bed.

I went straight for the lamp, flipping the switch to bathe the room in darkness. Then my hand found the center of his chest, the dusting of coarse hair that felt like sin against the steel of his body. With one slight push, his shoulders relaxed into the pillows.

Tobias's hands came to my thighs, skimming the scalloped hem of my sleep shorts. "Eva."

"You kissed me and now I can't sleep," I repeated, straddling his lap. My core rocked against the growing arousal beneath the sheet. "Kiss me again. Please."

He surged to capture my mouth. No questions. No hesitation. No foreplay. Tobias kissed me like I was the air in his lungs, the reason he survived. His tongue fluttering against my own as his hands lifted the sides of my top.

He bunched the cotton in his fists, lifting it higher and higher, tearing his mouth away for only the briefest moment to whip the tank over my head. Then his hands found my breasts, and my God, he was good with his hands.

Cupping. Squeezing. Rolling. My nipples were his personal instruments and he played them like a symphony.

My hips rolled against his, grinding and rubbing. I held his face to mine, his thick beard lightly scraping against my palms. The throb in my core bloomed. "Fuck me, Tobias."

He growled against my lips. Then with one fast move, he flipped me onto my back, pushing my knees apart. His deft fingers slipped beneath my shorts, pulling my panties aside, to stroke my glistening folds.

"Yes," I hissed as he latched on to my pulse and sucked. "More."

He kicked and shoved at the sheets, and as my hand traveled down his spine, I found nothing but skin. Tobias hadn't slept naked in college, but like the beard, I'd gladly take this change.

A finger slid into my core, curling toward the ache. Except it wasn't enough. I needed more. I needed him.

"Inside." I reached between us, fisting his shaft. Velvet and iron. Hot and hard. "Come inside."

"Not yet."

"Tobias—"

"Not. Yet." Each word was accentuated with the plunge of his finger. "I want to feel your pussy like this. Then with my tongue. Then I'll give you my cock."

He made good on his promise, working me into a frenzy with his hand before tearing off my shorts and panties. Then he dragged that glorious beard against the tender flesh of my inner thighs.

I hummed, my eyes falling closed, as a shudder raced through my veins. My hand found his silky, dark hair. My fingertips tangled into the strands as he did that tongue flutter, this time against my clit.

"Tobias." I moaned his name, over and over, as his mouth continued its delicious torture. A lick. A nip. A suck. My breath came in hitched gasps as he feasted until I trembled, head to toe.

My back arched off the bed, writhing as he held my hips in place. I was seconds away from a blinding release, just one more lick, when he disappeared.

He leaned away, looming above me on his knees. Moonlight streamed through the window, casting his body in light and shadow. The cut of his biceps. The peaks and valleys of his chest. The ripples of his abdomen.

Tobias was magnificent. He was mine.

He'd always been mine, even when I'd let him go.

I stretched a hand for his. He took it, lacing our fingers together, and raised it above his head. Then his lips crashed down on mine, and with one swift thrust, he planted deep.

I whimpered down his throat. I trembled beneath his strokes. Thrust after thrust, he held me captive until I had nothing left to do but fall. The orgasm shook my body in waves as I clenched around him.

"Fuck, babe." He gritted his teeth, his rhythm never slowing, as I rode out the aftershocks and let the stars fade from behind my eyes.

The sound of skin slapping, of heavy breaths and racing hearts, echoed in the room. Then he reared up, taking my knees, and holding me to him as he came, pouring inside me on a roar.

He came undone. Entirely. For me.

Tobias panted, taking a few moments to regain his breath. Then he ran a hand over his mouth before bending to kiss my cheek. "Damn. That was . . . it's always better. Every time."

"I know," I whispered, rising to kiss his mouth.

No one would compare to Tobias. Maybe that was why I'd never wanted another man. I didn't need experience to know, in my soul, that I'd already had the best.

He shifted and broke our connection, then curled my back into his chest.

"I can go back to my room," I said, hoping he wouldn't let me go.

Hoping he'd ask me to stay.

But he didn't voice the word. He never had. Instead, he held me closer and dragged the blankets over our naked bodies. "Good night, Eva."

I closed my eyes. "Good night, Tobias."

———

"KNOCK, KNOCK." I tapped on Dad's door and peered into his apartment.

He was in his recliner, asleep as the TV's muted volume did its best to drown out the sound of his snores.

I eased the door closed behind me and tiptoed into the room, taking up a seat on the couch.

Dad deserved to rest. He deserved mid-morning naps on New Year's Eve. And because of my job, he could have them.

So I took out my phone and played a trivia game while I waited. Or I tried to play a trivia game. Mostly I thought about last night with Tobias.

We hadn't spoken much this morning. I'd woken first, slipping out of his bed and heading to the shower. When I'd found him in the kitchen later, he'd been dressed for the day in a pair of jeans and a navy flannel.

He'd had work to do at the office, but he'd promised to

be home by dinner. Then we'd celebrate New Year's, assuming I could stay awake until midnight.

I had a feeling that he'd make sure I saw fireworks.

After an hour, Dad's snoring stopped and his eyes fluttered open.

"Hi, Dad." I smiled.

"Eva." He blinked twice, then hit the button on the chair to sit up straighter. "Sorry. I didn't know you were here."

"It's okay. I don't mind hanging out."

He smiled, the crooked smile I'd grown used to these past three years. "Last day?"

"Yep." I nodded. "Last day."

"I'm sure gonna miss you. I've been spoiled having you here so long this time. Did you see Elena?"

"I went over yesterday. And I'll miss you too." I opened my mouth to tell him I had news. That I was having a baby. But the announcement lodged in my throat.

Dad was a practical man. He'd taught us to love schedules and routine. As kids, the kitchen calendar had been marked with all of Mom's travel dates so we'd know where she was going and when she'd be home.

He'd ask questions about the baby. About how Tobias and I were going to handle parenting and if I'd keep doing my job.

If I was going to give him a string of *I don't knows*, we'd better get some food first.

"I was thinking we could go grab lunch," I said.

"Sure." He reached for his cane, pushing to his feet and taking a moment to get his balance.

We decided on a café in town, one I hadn't been to yet. We took our seats in a booth, ordered soup and sandwiches, then sipped our waters as we waited for our meals.

"So you're off again," Dad said, toying with his napkin.

"Yep." It was always difficult to leave Montana, but today, there was more bitter than sweet.

"Any idea when you can take a quick trip home to visit?"

"I'm not sure yet. Maybe in a month or two? Once I get there and get caught up on the build, I'll have a better idea."

"And what are you building this time?"

"A fulfillment center."

"Ah." He nodded. "Big?"

"Not as big as most. The logistics have been tricky. And the clients are, er . . . particular. But I'm up for the challenge."

"Of course you are." He grinned. "My girl never backs away from a challenge."

Was that why I was going? Because I was too stubborn to back away? Or because I genuinely liked the work?

"Can I ask you something about Mom?"

"Yeah. Go ahead." He nodded but there was tension in his shoulders. A tension I'd seen my entire life when Mom was brought into the conversation.

"Do you think I'm like her?" It was the question I'd wanted to ask for years but hadn't had the courage.

"You mean the travel?"

I nodded. "Yeah."

"No." He chuckled. "Not in the slightest."

"R-really?" Because when I looked in the mirror, I saw the similarities.

"Eva, your mom traveled to escape her life. Maybe it was because of me. We were never friends. I think she learned early on that when she came home, it wasn't to her house, but to mine. We didn't talk. We didn't laugh. We just coexisted. And I hate that you girls paid the price for our indifference."

My heart twisted, not for us, but for them. I knew what it was like to be in love with your best friend. Pure magic.

"Probably shouldn't be telling you this, but when you were two, we talked about a divorce," he said. "Michelle was worried that if she couldn't at least come home to you and Elena, you'd forget about her completely. So we worked out our arrangement. We agreed to stick it out until you graduated."

"That couldn't have been easy," I said.

"I've got a lot of pent-up resentment toward your mother. It wasn't easy and I guess . . . I think she could have tried harder to be home. To be a part of your lives. Instead, she took every trip they'd give her. She ran away from anything that resembled being tied down."

"Isn't that what I'm doing?" Guilt crept into my voice.

"Not even close." He stretched his good arm across the table, his hand covering mine. "You run and run and run. You take every task thrown your way and crush it like an empty pop can, destined for the recycling bin. But when you're ready to stop, you stop."

Was I ready to stop? It was coming. I felt fatigued, more and more each move.

"Mom was here a few days ago," I admitted.

"I know," he muttered. "She came to see me."

"What? She did? I didn't realize you kept in touch."

"Not often. But when she's in town, she stops by. We talk about you. We talk about Elena. She gets the details about you, a lot like she used to when you were younger. Then she goes on her way."

Acquaintances. That was how Mom lived her life, with acquaintances.

He gave me a sad smile. "For a long time, I wished that Michelle would just . . . love us. Love me. But I realized something years ago. She's not built to love deep. It's not in her makeup. But it is in yours."

I swallowed the lump in my throat, trying my best not to cry. "I hope you're right."

"Oh, I'm right." He picked up his spoon. "How's Tobias?"

I shook my head, letting out a dry laugh. *Well played, Dad.* "He's good. I, um, I actually have something important to tell you."

"You two getting back together?" It hurt to see such hope in his face. Dad had always loved Tobias.

"No. We're not. But we are, uh . . . having a baby?"

Dad blinked. Probably because I'd said it like a question. His spoon clattered on the table as it slipped from his hand.

"I'm pregnant." *Eeek.* "Surprise."

———

BY THE TIME I made it back to Tobias's house, I'd felt like I'd run a marathon. As expected, Dad had not been shy about the questions. He also hadn't been shy to tell me that *I'm not sure yet* and *we'll figure it out eventually* weren't real answers when it came to an infant.

I parked in the driveway, not the garage, and slipped the opener from the visor. The car wasn't mine, just a lease. Someone from the relocation company would pick it up from the airport parking lot tomorrow and I didn't want to forget Tobias's garage remote.

The snow was falling like white dust as I made my way inside, stomping my shoes on the doormat. The house smelled like Tobias's cologne. One breath and my shoulders sagged.

I would miss that smell. It was like . . . home.

Until tomorrow.

Like I'd done countless times, I packed my suitcase and readied it for travel. I made sure I had my passport and a book downloaded to my Kindle. I checked in for my flight and made sure I had my visa documentation handy. Then I retreated to the living room, curling up in the chair closest to the window.

The snow was falling heavier now. The yard was a blanket of smooth white bumps. Beyond the leafless trees, on the other side of Tobias's property, there was a hill. Not a big hill, but enough that a kid could go sledding on a day like this.

It was peaceful here. How had I not realized that before today? I didn't miss the city noise. I didn't miss the traffic or public transportation. I didn't miss crowded side-walks or loud neighbors. Tobias hadn't just built a home, but a sanctuary. His retreat.

Years ago, this house had been a napkin sketch. He probably didn't realize I remembered the night he'd drawn it out.

We'd been in my apartment, just the two of us, eating Chinese takeout. He'd doodled on a box first in blue pen before getting serious and pulling out a napkin. Four bedrooms. An office. Open concept with tall ceilings and a large kitchen. He'd wanted to live outside of town where he'd have an unobstructed view of the mountains. He'd wanted an abundance of windows so he could catch the sunrises and sunsets.

I loved that I'd been the first to hear about his dream home. I loved that he'd made that dream come true.

Snuggling deeper into the chair's cushions, I curled

my feet into the seat. I imagined a little girl with dark hair and blue eyes giggling as she made snow angels in the yard. Or maybe a little boy trying his best to build a snowman.

"Why hasn't he asked us to stay?" I whispered, sliding a hand across my belly.

The baby didn't have an answer.

Neither did I.

CHAPTER TEN

TOBIAS

I found Eva asleep in the chair. Her lips were slightly parted. Her knees were drawn in tight. One hand cradled her cheek while the other was splayed across her belly.

I'd been standing here for minutes, just watching. Hurting. Because goddamn it, I loved her.

I'd always loved her.

I always would.

And tomorrow, I'd watch her walk away. It was like having my heart broken all over again.

I rubbed a hand over my face, then forced myself out of the living room, retreating to my office. I spent the next three hours trying to think about anything but Eva and the baby, while outside the snow continued to fall, weighing heavy on the ground. Weighing heavy like my heart.

"Hey."

I looked up from my desk, finding Eva leaning against the doorframe. "Hey."

"I didn't realize how tired I was." She yawned. "Have you been back long?"

"A few hours."

Her gaze drifted past my shoulder to the windows. The house lights caught the snowflakes as they fell but beyond them it was dark. "It's black and white out there. I hope they don't cancel my flight tomorrow."

I couldn't say the same.

"Hungry?" I shoved out of my chair.

"Sure. I can cook."

"I'll do it. Keep me company." I escorted her to the kitchen, my hand at the small of her back.

If she was leaving, I might as well touch her while I could. The next time we saw each other, she might not want my hands on her. Maybe she never would again.

Eva sat at the island, on her stool, while I got to work making a pasta dish. "So we should talk."

"Yeah." I put a pot of water on the stove to boil. "Probably should."

"I was thinking—" The chime of her phone cut through the room. "Sorry."

She slid off her seat and answered. "Hello?"

I took out some vegetables and sausage from the fridge, working and listening as she spoke.

"Shoot." She sighed. "Well, at least I'll be there soon. First thing Monday morning, I'll meet with them, and see if I can't smooth things out. Forward me their email. I'll review it on my flight."

Eva paced the length of the island as she listened, worrying her bottom lip between her teeth. Then she nodded. "Talk to you then. Bye."

"Trouble?" I asked as she returned to her stool.

"That was my boss. The clients for this project aren't exactly easy to work with. At the moment, they're frustrated that the build isn't moving as quickly as they'd like. They just sent a nasty email threatening to bring in their lawyer if we didn't show some visible progress in the next thirty days. My boss is a great guy, but emails like that send him into a tailspin."

"No build ever happens as quickly as a client wants."

"True. But it will be fine. Once I get there, build a rapport and they see some progress, we'll win them over."

She would win them over. "Of that, I have no doubt."

Eva loved a challenge. One semester in college, she'd signed up for twenty-three credits, adding an extra class than normal. It had been a lot of work, but she'd had this determination not to fail. She'd aced them all.

"What's been your favorite project?" I asked.

"Probably the one in Phoenix."

I focused on making our meal while she told me stories about her favorite assignments. Then I handed her a plate, taking the space beside her and raising my glass of sparkling grape juice for a toast.

"Cheers."

She clinked her glass to mine. "Cheers."

"It's interesting hearing you talk about your buildings," I said as we ate. "You love them because of the clients or the foremen. I love mine because of the actual structure."

"I mean . . . there's not a lot to love about boring, boxy buildings. So yeah, usually the ones that stand out are because I like the people."

"Do you keep in touch with them?"

"Not really. It's hard after I leave. By the time I actually meet friends, it's usually close to the time I'm about to go. We drift apart."

"Sorry."

She shrugged, swirling her fork in her penne. "It can get lonely. That's my only complaint. There are days when I feel like I'm on an island. But then I call home and talk to Elena or Dad, and remember that I'll always have them."

"And me. You'll have me."

Her eyes softened. "Thank you."

"So . . . before your call, you were going to say something."

"Oh, just that I've been thinking. Maybe we could pick a long weekend for you to come to London. If you can get away. Once I get there, I'll find a doctor. We could time the trip with an appointment."

"Yeah." It was a totally reasonable idea. Totally fucking reasonable. But it set me on edge, and my fingers gripped my fork too tight.

"And then I can come here. I can make a few trips while it's still okay for me to travel."

Until no doctor would let her on an airplane and she'd be half a world away. Who knew when she'd go into labor? Who'd take her to the hospital? Who'd be there to make sure she didn't lift anything too heavy?

I let go of the fork before I bent the metal and fisted my hand on the island. "But you'll be here to have the baby. You said your project would be six to eight months, right?"

"Um, maybe? The project might . . . take longer."

"What?" I clipped. Where the hell had this come from? Why hadn't she mentioned that earlier this week?

"It could take up to a year."

I blinked. "A year?"

What happened when she went into labor? What if it happened too fast and I couldn't make it there in time?

I shoved off my stool, dragging a hand through my hair as I walked around the island. Sitting side by side wasn't working. I needed to look at her face and make sure I had this right. "So you're going to have the baby in London."

"Given the timing, probably. Yes. I doubt my doctor will want me flying to Montana during my third trimester."

"Then what? Maternity leave?"

"Depends on the project. I'll have to talk to my boss. He might want to send someone out to help by that point.

But if it's going well, then I might be able to just work from home. Do occasional site visits."

"Is it an option? Finding someone else to do this job?"

She sat up straighter. "Maybe. I'd rather not ask."

"What about finding you a job closer to Montana?"

"Again, I'd rather not ask. I want to do this London project."

"You won't ask your boss to assign you to a job in America. But you'll ask me to fly back and forth, hopefully with enough notice that I can be there for the birth of my child. And then what? You get a new assignment? You pack up and go somewhere else?"

"I don't know." She climbed off her stool, pacing on one side of the island while I did the same on the opposite. "I don't know. Okay? I'm just now wrapping my brain around the fact that I'm growing a human. I haven't exactly figured out how I'm going to raise him or her yet."

"You can't."

She gasped, her feet stopping. "What?"

"This can't be the life you want for our child. Traveling all over. Bouncing from school to school."

"It might not be like that."

"Then you'll quit your job?"

"I don't know." She tossed up her hands. "Do I have to have the answers today?"

"No, but a goddamn direction would be good. I have to know what you're thinking. I have to know what you're going to sacrifice. I have to know that you're not going to be like your mother." I regretted it the moment I spoke. *Fuck.*

Eva gasped. "I can't believe you just said that to me. Why have all our conversations been about my sacrifices? What about you?"

"Me?" I pointed to my chest. "I have a steady job. I am taking over my father's company. I have a house. A fucking address. You really think I'm going to give that up? We both know that the right place for this kid to grow up is here. With me."

Eva's eyes widened. Her mouth fell open. "What?"

"It makes sense. If you keep your job, then the baby should live here."

The air in the room went still. The only sound was my racing heart. Eva stared at me and my biggest fear came to life.

There was nothing but disdain in her eyes. Nothing but resentment.

She hated me.

And if there was a piece of my heart left that she hadn't broken the first time, it shattered in that very moment.

Except I couldn't even blame her. This one . . . this one was on me.

"An ultimatum," she whispered, her eyes flooding. "I can't believe you just gave me an ultimatum. You know what I wished for earlier? That you'd ask me to stay."

My heart stopped.

"But you didn't. Not before. Not now. You've never asked me to stay." And judging by the tone in her voice, now it was too late.

"You broke my fucking heart."

"Then I guess tonight makes us even." She swallowed hard. "Happy New Year, Tobias."

The sound of her slamming door echoed through the house. I stood frozen, immobilized by the pain.

She hated me.

To be fair, tonight, I sort of hated myself.

CHAPTER ELEVEN

EVA

My eyes were puffy and the circles beneath them blue. Splotchy cheeks and pale lips weren't a good look for me. This wasn't exactly how I'd hoped to start my new year, crying through the midnight hours and barely sleeping. But at least I could nap on the plane.

I stretched a hair tie around my wrist, then took one last look in the mirror. Yep, I looked like crap. The last time I'd looked this awful had been years ago. This was the face I'd worn for weeks after moving to New York.

It was like the heartache was so immense that it couldn't stay inside. It blanched my skin. It hollowed my cheeks. It sat like a chimney of bricks upon my shoulders.

Tobias's ultimatum rang through my mind. It made it hard to see straight because the worst part was . . .

He was right.

I was clinging to a foolish hope that my life wouldn't

have to change. But nothing about my life was normal. I couldn't drag a baby around with me from city to city. I couldn't keep my job and be a mother.

He was right. I knew he was right. I'd known it for a week.

Yet last night, even after all those words, he hadn't asked me to stay. He wanted the baby. Just not me.

I swiped at my cheeks, sniffling the sting out of my nose. Then I steeled my spine, pulled on my coat and collected my suitcase. No, I couldn't work forever, at least not in the same capacity. But I wasn't quitting today. I wasn't quitting tomorrow.

I'd go to London, give myself time to mourn the loss of my career, then formulate an exit plan. It was time to update my résumé.

With my suitcase dragging behind me, I looped my backpack strap over a shoulder and left Tobias's guest bedroom behind. Would he turn it into the baby's nursery?

I clenched my jaw to keep the emotion from bubbling free as I marched down the hallway.

The scent of coffee greeted me in the kitchen. Tobias stood at the sink, his back to me as he stared out the window overlooking his backyard.

Would he put a swing set out there? Or maybe a playhouse? Would he make this home a child's paradise so that I had no chance of competing?

Tobias turned, his eyes darted to my bags. "I'll help you load up."

"I can do it." I raised my chin. "Thanks for letting me crash here this week. I stripped the bed. Towels are in the hamper."

He nodded. "Appreciate it."

My heart hammered three beats for every step toward the front door. I twisted the knob, but before I could step outside, my suitcase was tugged free from my hand.

Tobias stood there, so close I could smell his cologne. I drew it in, holding it for a long moment, then exhaled.

He followed close behind as I walked into the cold, my breath billowing in a white cloud as I crossed the clean sidewalk. He must have shoveled while I'd been in the shower. He'd also cleaned the snow from my car.

I hit the button for the trunk, stepping aside so he could load my suitcase. Then I tossed in my backpack and met his gaze.

Those blue eyes were like sapphires, glittering in the morning sun. His Adam's apple bobbed as he swallowed. "Call me."

"I will."

He studied me, the dark circles and dull skin, his forehead furrowing. "Eva, I—"

"Don't." My voice trembled. "Please don't. I need to get going."

And I was hanging on by a thread. I couldn't fight with him, not again.

"All right." He moved, shifting out of my way so we

wouldn't touch as I brushed past him and hurried for the driver's side door.

I slid inside, the cold from the seat seeping through my jeans.

Tobias braced his hands on the roof, bending as I inserted the key into the ignition. "I'm sorry. For what it's worth, what I said last night, I'm sorry."

The tears threatened, so I simply nodded and turned the key. "Goodbye, Tobias."

His hands fell to his sides and he stepped away. "Goodbye, Eva."

Another miserable farewell.

I didn't let myself look at him as I reversed out of the driveway. I didn't let myself glance in the rearview mirror as my tires crunched on the fresh snow of his lane. I didn't let myself think that there'd been regret on his face as he'd said goodbye.

This week had been an epic clusterfuck, from that stupid song to last night's fight.

I should have stayed in my empty condo. We should have maintained boundaries. Too much time had passed for us to be jumping into bed together. He might know me better than anyone, but that didn't mean I was the same young woman I'd been in college.

We'd drifted apart. We'd become different people.

And now, we'd have to figure out a way to become parents.

The miles to the airport passed in a blur. My focus

was nonexistent, but there was a plus side to moving and traveling so often. I maneuvered the airport with mechanical ease, checking my baggage and navigating security. Most of the chairs outside the gate were full, but I found an empty seat next to a window.

There was an older couple seated across from me. I met the woman's gaze and it was so full of pity that I winced. Okay, maybe I looked worse than crap. The flight attendants would probably ask if I was all right.

I forced a tight smile at the woman, then twisted sideways in the seat, folding my legs toward my chest so I could look outside.

The ground crew was busy loading suitcases onto a conveyor belt. One man in a neon vest was waving two orange wands. Mom had taught us years ago how pilots navigated runway lines and markers.

What airport would she be flying to today? Did she ever feel sad coming to this airport? Because I did. Every single time.

I stared at the workers, keeping my eyes aimed through the glass as the tears began to fall.

This was just so goddamn familiar. This was just like the day I'd left for New York.

I was in a blue, vinyl chair again. I was crying at the Bozeman airport again. I was staring at a Boeing 737 with a heart torn to confetti.

My hand found my belly. I pressed it close, squeezing shut my eyes.

Was I making a huge mistake? Would I regret this decision?

Before New York, there hadn't been a scrap of hesitation in my mind. Yes, I'd been devastated and broken about Tobias, but when the gate agent had called my row, I'd stood tall, dried my face and walked down the sky bridge.

Today's doubts were paralyzing. They kept me pinned to my chair, even as my name was called. Even as the plane taxied down the runway.

Even as it took flight without me.

CHAPTER TWELVE

TOBIAS

The pencil in my hand snapped in half. That was the third one this morning. The graphite line on my sketch made it unusable so I crumpled it in a fist and tossed it toward the trash.

"Damn it." I shoved out of my chair and stormed from the office. What was the point in working? I couldn't fucking concentrate, and I was so tense that my office supplies were paying the price.

I checked my phone again. Eva had been gone for two hours. She was probably at the airport, about to get on her flight. Was she okay? This morning she'd looked tired and pissed and . . . hurt.

This was why I'd never wanted to fight with her. Because it made me feel like I was crawling out of my skin.

I pulled up her name in my phone, my fingers hovering over the keyboard to send her a text. But what was I supposed to say? I'm sorry? Yeah, I'd tried that this morning.

Travel safe.

I typed it. I deleted it.

Miss you.

Type. Delete.

Stay.

Type.

Delete.

It was too late. After our fight, I'd all but shoved her out the door. Besides, if she was going to stay, it had to be her decision.

Maybe it was a good thing that we wouldn't see each other for a couple of months. Maybe by then our feelings wouldn't be as raw. She'd be settled in London and might have a better idea how long this job would take.

I'd just have to wait.

My hands fisted. Months? No way. I'd turned myself inside out in just an hour. How could I endure months?

The house, my sanctuary, felt empty this morning. Soon, her scent would vanish. I'd forget how it looked when she sat at the island. I'd miss having her next to me on the couch for Hallmark movies.

Was this really a home if my heart was on its way to London?

The stomp of footsteps on the stoop caught my ear, followed by the doorbell. Was it Eva? Had she come back? I flew toward the door and ripped it open.

"Hey." Maddox jerked up his chin.

My shoulders fell. "Hi."

"Hoping I was someone else?"

"Eva." I waved him inside. "She left this morning."

"For London?" he asked, unzipping his coat.

"Yeah." I tucked my hands in my pockets, then pulled them free. I dragged my palm over my cheek, then through my hair. If I didn't move, I felt like I'd explode. "What's up?"

"Just came by to check on you."

I blinked. "Why?"

Maddox chuckled. "Because I'm your brother. And by the looks of it, I came just in time. You keep rubbing your beard like that, you won't have to worry about shaving."

"Huh? Oh." I dropped my hand from my jaw. It went into my pocket and came right back out.

"Talk to me." Maddox clapped a hand on my shoulder, tugging me toward the living room. He steered me to the chair while he sat on the edge of the couch. "You guys talk about the baby?"

"Yeah." I was seated for a whole five seconds before I rose to my feet. "We got in a fight last night. I told her I thought that the baby should live here with me since she travels all over."

Maddox cringed. "How'd that go?"

"Not good."

"What did she say when you asked her if she'd consider staying in Montana?"

"I, uh, didn't ask."

"What? Why not?" He stared at me like I'd grown two heads.

"Because it's complicated."

He leaned deeper into the couch, tossing an arm over the backrest. "I've got time for complicated."

I blew out a long breath. "I don't want her to stay because I asked. I want her to stay because she wants to stay. Because she wants me."

"That's fair."

I paced the length of the fireplace, my heart in my throat. Did she want me? Maybe she would have before yesterday? But after last night . . .

"She's the one," I confessed. "Always has been."

"You don't think she feels the same?"

"I don't know," I whispered. "Once, yes. But then I asked her to marry me, and well . . . we aren't married."

Maddox's mouth fell open. "Wait. You proposed? When?"

"Graduation."

"No one told me that."

"Because I didn't tell anyone. You're the first person I've told. It was, um . . . humiliating."

"I can imagine. But we would have understood. We would have been there."

"I know," I muttered. "I think part of the reason I didn't tell anyone was that I was protecting Eva. I don't want anyone to hate her. Especially Mom."

Maddox leaned forward, bracing his elbows on his knees. "So you didn't ask her to stay because you're worried she'd turn you down again."

I tapped my nose. "It'll be fine. We'll figure this out. I was working on some sketches for your place. Want to see them?"

"No." He scoffed. "I don't give a damn about the house. You're not fine, Tobias."

No, I wasn't.

My chest felt too tight. My limbs weak. "I don't know what to do. I want to be there for her. For the baby."

"You have to tell her how you feel. If you want her to stay, ask. Maybe she'll surprise you."

Maybe she would. She'd basically said that last night, hadn't she? Or had I just heard what I'd wanted to hear? Our conversation was becoming a blur and the growing throb behind my temples wasn't helping.

"What if she doesn't?"

"Then you know," he said. "You can let her go."

Would I ever let Eva go? "Well, I'm sort of fucked at the moment. She's on her way to London."

"And?"

I gave him a sideways glance. "And, what? I work here. My home is here. Once I get a break in my schedule, I'll plan a trip or something."

"Or you could go today." Maddox stood and rounded the coffee table to stand in front of me. "Family first,

Tobias. Take it from a man who has struggled with that concept. You'll regret anything else."

"I am picking family. Mom. Dad. Heath. Now you're moving home."

"We'll always be family. But we're not *your* family. Yours. The one you're making. I love Mom and Dad. You and Heath. But *my* family is Violet. And for my daughter, there's nothing I wouldn't do."

My family. There was only one person I wanted to build that with. "Shit."

"Yep."

"I need to get to the airport."

"Let's go." He strode for the door, swiping his jacket from the hook.

I ran to grab my keys and wallet from the kitchen counter, doing a frantic scan around the house. What else did I need? Clothes? Toiletries?

"Passport," Maddox ordered like he could read my mind.

"Right." I jogged to the safe in my walk-in closet, punching in the code. With my passport in hand, I left the rest behind. There were stores in London. I could snag necessities like a toothbrush and soap on a layover.

I passed the dresser, thinking I could at least shove a clean pair of boxers and socks in my coat pocket. I ripped open the top drawer and froze. There was only one thing I needed.

A ring. Maybe I'd kept it all these years because, deep

down, I'd hoped for a second chance to put it on Eva's finger.

I pulled on a coat and put the box in the pocket closest to my heart. Maddox was already in his SUV when I stepped into the cold. The moment I was in my seat, he tore out of the driveway and down the road.

"My jet is in a hangar," he said. "Do you know her flight itinerary? When she touches down in London?"

"No. I'm guessing she's off to Seattle first." I frantically switched between airline apps, checking my options. "There's a flight there in an hour. Then a three-hour layover."

There were only two flights from Seattle to London today. Hopefully I picked the right one. Hopefully she was going to Seattle first, not Denver or Salt Lake.

"My pilot will fly you to Heathrow. You'd only have to stop for fuel."

"But if I can catch up to her, then I'll be on her flight to London." Even if she was pissed at me, we'd be on the same plane. "Let me see what I can do when we get to the airport."

He nodded and hit the gas pedal.

We parked in the loading zone, Maddox not caring if he was towed. He stuck right by my side as I ran to a clerk and begged her to find me a flight to London.

Her nails were long and they clacked against the keyboard as she typed. Then a slow smile spread across her face. "You're on the next flight to Seattle. Then I've got you on the connection to London. There's one seat left. It's not cheap."

I passed her my credit card. "Book it."

"Call if you get stranded," Maddox said. "I'll send my pilot to pick you up."

"Thanks."

He grinned. "Go get her."

"I will." My heart raced. This was happening. I was leaving it all behind to chase my woman.

And with every cell in my body, I knew it was the right choice.

With a wave, my brother started for the doors, but I stopped him before he could get too far.

"Maddox?"

He turned. "Yeah?"

"Glad you're home."

"Me too." One more wave and then he weaved through people before he disappeared outside.

The clerk handed me my tickets and I bolted from the desk, taking the stairs toward security two at a time. I stripped off my belt and fumbled to remove my shoes. Then I waited in line, shifting my weight between my feet, as the four people ahead of me walked through the scanner at a snail's pace.

Come on. I was in a hurry to get to my gate and . . . wait.

Adrenaline coursed through my veins and the pace

was torture. But finally, I was marching through the terminal.

I scanned the displays, making sure I was heading toward the right place. I passed an empty seating area, seeing only one person against the glass. Her legs were tucked into the chair as she stared outside and across the runway. Her red coat hugged her slight frame.

My steps slowed.

I knew that red coat.

"What the—" I changed direction, moving straight toward the window. Was this real? "Eva?"

She jerked, whipping toward my voice. Her hazel eyes were full of tears. "Tobias?"

"I thought your flight was at ten."

"It was." She wiped furiously at her cheeks, sitting straight. "I missed it."

Was that why she was crying? "There's another one in an hour."

"Oh. I'll try—wait. How do you know that? What are you doing here?"

I sat in the chair beside hers. "Taking the flight to Seattle in an hour. Then making a connection to London."

"What?"

"Why'd you miss your flight?"

She lifted a shoulder. "I'm stuck."

I took her right hand in mine, curling our fingers together. Then I tapped my thumb across her index finger. "One. Two. Three. Four."

She sniffled. "I declare a thumb war."

"Shake." Our thumbs touched. "Winner asks the first question."

She didn't even put up a fight and my thumb trapped hers instantly.

"Why are you stuck?"

"Because I'm not sure if I'm making a huge mistake."

"Go again." We did another thumb duel, again she let me win.

"Do you want to go to London?"

"No. Yes." Her eyes flooded. "I don't know."

"How about if I go with you?"

Her chin quivered. "Really?"

"Really. If I went with you to London, would you want to go?"

"Yes. But . . . then what?"

"I don't know, babe." I let her hand go to frame her face. "I don't know. But we could start with this trip. Then the next. What I know is that I can't let you go. So if that means I go with you, then here I am."

"Tobias, I—" She shook her head. "What are you saying?"

"I love you."

Another tear dropped. "I love you too."

I slammed my lips onto hers, swallowing a moan. Her tears continued to fall, dripping onto my face, but as I kissed her, she started laughing, clinging to me as I clung to her until a throat cleared from the gate agent tore us apart.

"You'd really go to London with me?"

"I'm not going to ask you to stay," I said. "Not because I don't want you to stay, but because I think you would. You'd stay for me and the baby even though you're not ready. You want London. So London is what we'll do."

"I would stay."

Yeah, she would. But I wouldn't make her choose. I wasn't going to be the man who smothered her dreams and delivered ultimatums. She deserved better. "How about one more adventure? We tackle London. Then we'll decide what's next. Together."

"Are you sure? What about your home? Your family?"

I tucked a lock of hair behind her ear. "I'm looking at my family. I'm staring at my home."

"I haven't had a home, a real one, in a long time."

"You do now." I kissed her forehead, then took her hand again. "Thumb wrestle to see who gets my first-class ticket."

She gave me a wicked grin. There'd be no letting me win this time. "You're on."

EPILOGUE

EVA

One year later . . .

"Since we're early, can we swing by a project site real quick?" Tobias asked as I drove us toward town. "I want to see how the exterior lights look at night."

"Sure. Which way?"

"At the stop sign, head north."

"Whoa." I shot him a scowl. "Watch your language."

"What?"

"You said north."

He chuckled, shaking his head. "Take a left at the stop sign."

"Better." I smirked, then cast my eyes to the rearview.

Isabella was asleep in her car seat, her tiny lips in a perfect pout. This would be a long night for her, considering it was already past her bedtime.

Tonight was the annual Holiday family Christmas

party and she was dressed for the occasion. Her red velvet dress was trimmed with white. Her slippers wouldn't last because she hated shoes but I'd put them on over her tights regardless.

"Did you grab the earmuffs?" Tobias asked.

"Yes," I muttered. Those freaking earmuffs. "They're in the diaper bag."

His parents had hired a live band, like they did most years, and it was going to get loud at the venue. So Tobias had found a pair of baby-sized earmuffs. Except instead of finding a cute pink or purple pair, heaven forbid something that would coordinate with her dress, he'd found orange.

Hunter's orange.

When I'd asked him why he'd picked such a heinous color, he'd told me they'd been the only ones with adjustments so she could wear them as she grew older.

My husband was nothing if not practical.

Tobias had proposed to me outside a women's restroom in the Seattle airport. The charmer. In all fairness, I'd botched his plans for something romantic. I'd leaned my head against his chest, and when my cheek had hit something hard in his coat pocket, I'd pestered him to tell me what he was carrying until he'd finally caved.

The same ring he'd bought years ago had been on my finger ever since. And as of last week, there was a wedding band to keep it company.

We'd gotten married the day after we'd finally moved

home to Montana. The two of us had gone to the courthouse over lunch and made it official.

No dress. No tux. Just Tobias, our daughter and me.

It hadn't taken me long into the London project to realize I wasn't up for another move. By my third trimester, when my ankles had been swollen and my back had ached and the heartburn had been unbearable, all I'd wanted was to go home.

To Montana.

Dad had been right. I'd needed to run and run. But when I'd been ready to stop, we'd stopped. We'd waited for Isabella to join the world, then when she was old enough, we'd moved out of our London flat and flown home.

Hannah and Keith were overjoyed to have us close. They'd kept watch over our house while we'd been gone, keeping it clean and fresh for our visits home this past year. They'd even flown to see us once. And Keith had made sure that Tobias had been able to continue his work, hiring another architect for Holiday Homes. So while Tobias had drafted plans from afar, there'd been someone in Bozeman to act as boots on the ground and help see the projects through.

"Okay, left here." He pointed out the windshield, directing us through a maze of roads until we pulled up to a house that stood proudly in a snow-covered field.

"Wow."

"Turned out well."

"That's an understatement, baby." I took his hand, smiling as I stared at the home.

The owners had wanted a barn-style house with a gable roof and sliding front door. When he'd told me about it, I'd been skeptical, but leave it to Tobias to create something enchanting and unique.

A small whimper from the backseat meant we needed to keep driving, so I took my foot off the brake of my new SUV and headed into town.

The Baxter Hotel was like a golden beacon, standing tall on Main Street. The moment we stepped into the ballroom on the second floor, we were mobbed by friends and family here to welcome us home.

Then the band started and Tobias instantly retrieved the earmuffs.

"Could you have picked a different color?" Hannah asked as he fit them over Isabella's head.

"What's wrong with orange?" he asked.

I rolled my eyes. "It doesn't go."

"She's a baby. She doesn't care." He lifted Isabella from my arms, kissing her cheek, then set her in her favorite place in the world—the crook of his arm.

I'd fallen in love with Tobias years ago, but watching him with our daughter was like falling all over again.

"Let's dance." He clasped my hand, dropping a chaste kiss to my mouth, then steered us through the crowd to the dance floor. With the baby in one arm, he swept me into the other.

"I'm glad we could be here for this." I rested my head against his shoulder as we swayed. "And for Christmas."

"Me too," he murmured. "No regrets?"

"None."

My boss hadn't been happy when I'd told him that London would be my last project. He'd offered me a huge raise to stay on but I'd turned him down. Because I'd already found another job.

After New Year's, I'd be joining the crew at Holiday Homes as their newest project manager. I'd be working for the family business.

There was a chance that Tobias and I would kill each other, working in the same office. Or there was a chance we'd have quickies on the regular after hours.

We'd figure it out. Together.

"How about a holiday classic?" the band's lead singer asked into the microphone as they rounded out a song. "We've been doing this sing-a-long all year and it's a blast. What do you say?"

The room erupted into cheers of agreement.

And then the lead guitarist began to play. "On the first day of Christmas, my true love gave to me."

I glanced at Tobias.

He threw his head back and laughed.

Then we sang along. And at the end, when we got to our version, we both changed the lyrics.

Two turtle doves,

And a partridge and a pregnancy.

THE NAUGHTY, THE NICE AND THE NANNY

One week with one little girl—an angel, according to my staffing agency. Acting as the short-term nanny for a single dad should have been an easy way to make some extra cash. Until I show up for my first day and face off with a demon disguised as a seven-year-old girl wearing a red tutu and matching glitter slippers.

Oh, and her father? My temporary boss? Maddox Holiday. The same Maddox Holiday I crushed on in high school. The same Maddox Holiday who didn't even know I existed. And the same Maddox Holiday who hasn't set foot in Montana for years because he's been too busy running his billionaire empire.

Enduring seven days is going to feel like scaling the Himalayas in six-inch heels. Toss in the Holiday family's annual soiree, and Christmas Eve nightmares really do come true. But I can do anything for a week, especially for this paycheck, even if it means wrangling the naughty, impressing the nice, and playing the nanny.

THREE BELLS, TWO BOWS AND ONE
BROTHER'S BEST FRIEND

I pride myself in being grounded. Sure, I've had my share of childhood fantasies. Winning an Oscar. Winning the lottery. Winning an Olympic medal for an athletic talent I have yet to discover. But the only fantasy I ever thought might actually happen was winning my brother's best friend.

Heath Holiday.

My crush on him has ebbed and flowed over the years, but the day I started working for his construction company was the day I smothered it for good. Sort of. Mostly. It was on my to-do list. Making it a priority would have been easier had he not arrived at his family's annual Christmas party looking ridiculously handsome in a suit.

Then he kissed me. We stepped into an alternate universe and he kissed me. I assumed the next day I'd just be Guy's little sister again. The office newbie. Our kiss forgotten. Except he keeps showing up at my house. With gifts.

A gold bracelet carrying three jingling bells. Two dainty jeweled earrings, each shaped as a bow. And finally, he brought himself.

One brother's best friend, asking if I can keep a secret.

ACKNOWLEDGMENTS

Happy Holidays! I hope this book was as fun for you to read as it was for me to write. On a whim, I decided last Christmas to write three stories for this Christmas. I dragged it out over the course of months because that Christmas cheer was such a joy to add to my every day.

A huge thanks to my editing and proofreading team: Marion, Karen, Judy and Julie. Thank you to Sarah Hansen for the cutest covers in the world. Thanks to my agent, Kimberly, and the team at Brower Literary. And my publicist, Nina, and the team at Valentine PR.

Thanks to the members of Perry and Nash. I'm not sure how I got so lucky to have such an incredible reader group for both my Devney Perry and my Willa Nash books, but know that your love and support mean the world to me.

The same is true for the amazing bloggers who read and promote my stories. I am so grateful for you all!

And lastly, thanks to Bill, Will and Nash. I wrote these books in the evenings and love that you let me take an hour here and there to play with these characters.

ABOUT THE AUTHOR

Willa Nash is *USA Today* Bestselling Author Devney Perry's alter ego, writing contemporary romance stories for Kindle Unlimited. Lover of Swedish Fish, hater of laundry, she lives in Washington State with her husband and two sons. She was born and raised in Montana and has a passion for writing books in the state she calls home.

Don't miss out on Willa's latest book news.
Subscribe to her newsletter!
www.willanash.com